WHOSE EYES ARE THESE?

MARCIA BYALICK

BLACK ROSE
writing™

ISBN: 978-1-61296-463-8

PUBLISHED BY BLACK ROSE WRITING

www.blackrosewriting.com

Printed in the United States of America

Suggested retail price $14.95

Whose Eyes are These? is printed in Adobe Caslon Pro

To Hannah and Matthew who brighten my every day...

There are times I think I can't possibly love you more.

And then I do.

ACKNOWLEDGMENTS

I am indebted to the bright ideas and sharp eyes of my oh-so-intelligent and loving readers...Barbara, Debra, Judy, Nanette and Jane.

Special thank you to Jennifer, Carrie, Karen and Susan who insisted every step of the way the book was good, I was good and I could do it.

And to those who once rejected this book, thank you for forcing me to do better.

WHOSE EYES

ARE THESE?

CHAPTER ONE

When I think back to the moment right before life as I knew it officially ended, I can't believe all the stupid stuff I let bother me. So I spilled ketchup on my new sweater at lunch, and got a B- on my math test, big deal. All it takes is uncovering one secret... so earth shaking, so never ending in its consequences, and so unordinary that not one person you ever met could begin to understand... to realize how few things are worth getting upset about.

As usual Emma was humming all through dinner, inhaling Mom's boring baked chicken as if it were a bacon cheeseburger. I don't know about you but I find few things more irritating than an eight year old who snacks happily on baby carrots and somehow never manages to finish dessert.

"I want to change my name," she announced dramatically. She pushed her dish away and sat back on her knees to insure we understood how serious she was. If I ever tried sitting like that at the dinner table when I was in third grade, my parents would have made me put my legs down and sit straight. It seemed to me that child rearing rules really relaxed during the four years separating us... or maybe just in my house.

"Emma's an OK name," she continued, "but I like Lara better."

"Lara? Where did you get that name from?" chuckled my father.

She got off her chair and climbed on Dad's lap. "Miss Ullman told us today that she thought Lara was a beautiful name," she said mournfully, lying her head back on his shoulder, "and I think so too."

Oh please, I thought, shoot me. Now don't get me wrong, I'm proud of my sister. She, like my father, is a great athlete; her swimming and soccer awards already equaled the number of trophies he won as football coach of Kennedy High School. And it wasn't a sibling rivalry thing... how can a 12 year old and an eight year old be rivals? No, it was a matter of fairness. If a meal took 30 minutes, and there were two children present, you don't need to be a Supreme Court Justice to understand that sometimes I was entitled to five minutes to discuss my life.

Especially when the next day, before first period, it was my turn to audition for the position of dance captain in the seventh grade talent show. I took ballet and jazz since second grade and got into hip hop two years ago when my dance teacher suggested it. It was my favorite thing to do. As their conversation continued, I started fiddling with my fingernails, clicking them against each other, tapping out the combinations I would show Mr. Altman.

I had worked hard on my choreography. My best friend Molly and I u-tubed the coolest hip hop dances, then watched them over and over, imitating the ones we liked best. I'd break down every combination into counts of eight. Molly said that each combination was like a sentence in a song. The eighth beat is usually the end of the sentence, when we'd feel a new section of the song coming up, sort of like in a chorus.

I'd combine a neck roll from one dance with a hand movement I picked from another. By the time the whole routine came together, it had a hundred parts that became totally my own creation. I'd start with arms raised and bent at the elbows, fists clenched. Next a swizzle to the side, head snap, right hand clutching left arm. Then arms down, head too, in a kind of crawl. Fast paced but still flowing, that was the goal. In a second I was miles away from feeling angry. That was one of the advantages of loving dance so much.

I knew the steps weren't as important as the energy I put into making them come alive. I just had to let it ooze out from my body, like it was second nature. Although I knew my parents secretly believed hip hop is mostly angry in-your-face gangsters yelling third grade poetry about sex and drugs, I had to give them credit. They trusted I would choose songs that made sense in my life… music with a message about freedom and respect. I couldn't wait till they saw what I was working on.

A moment later Dad let Emma down and brought his dish to the sink. I got up to join him, scraping the sticky remnants of dinner into the garbage. As we stood face to face, I was surprised to realize I was barely an inch shorter than he was. If the same thought crossed his mind, he'd probably think it was too bad I didn't play basketball.

As if he read my thoughts and sought to prove me wrong, he said, "You're lookin' long and lean, Sloane. More like a real dancer every day."

Praise from my dad always sounder louder than praise from my mom. I smiled.

Then the conversation shifted gears.

"Oh, Neil, don't forget your doctor's appointment tomorrow. I'll meet you there at 9:45," my mom said. "No excuses, so don't even try," she went on, noting his look of annoyance.

"Why does Dad have to go to the doctor?" I asked.

"When you change insurance policies, some companies require a physical examination," my father snapped. "It's just a big waste of time."

"And," added Mom, speaking to him but directing her voice at Emma and me, "Dad's going to ask the doctor why his glands have been swollen for almost a month now."

"It's nothing," grumbled Dad, impatient with the thought of being in less than perfect health, "I probably got hit with a ball."

He hated anything to do with doctors. Once he went to the emergency room for stitches after being hit in the eye playing racquetball. Another time he separated his shoulder. But I never remember him being sick.

"You got hit with a ball under your arm? I don't think so," said Mom, shaking her head. "Just ask him to take a look, that's all," she said firmly.

Dad leaned over to tickle Emma.

"Promise me you'll ask," she continued, not letting him off the hook till she heard him agree.

"OK, OK," Dad said tightly. "I'll ask him. Are we done talking about this now?"

"Sure, sweetheart," Mom said, walking around the table to plant a kiss on his forehead.

"Eat something," my mother begged as I raced out the door early the next morning. "You need fuel to dance. Just take a bite of a banana."

I knew she meant well but like most mothers, she didn't get the ridiculousness of food lectures at certain moments in life.

"Fine," I said, grabbing the banana and kissing her good bye. We both pretended I would eat it on the way to school.

At 8:00 Mr. Altman was already waiting in the gym. He watched from his seat on a folding chair as I threw down my book bag, pulled back my hair and retied my sneakers. I handed him my Beats Pill and phone. When he saw what I chose to dance to, an ancient favorite, Missy Elliot's *Pass That Dutch*, he smiled approvingly. As the head of the music department, he respected that hip hop's roots came from Africa, China and Brazil. You could tell he enjoyed listening to Jay Z and Usher as much as we did.

He turned on the speaker and made it loud.. My back straightened and my ears grew longer as I imagined myself a figure on one of those Egyptian friezes we learned about in Global History. Automatically my body began to move. I concentrated hard on the combination, knowing the lower I kept to the floor, the easier it was to look breezy. Almost immediately my shirt clung to my back with sweat. That was one thing I did have in common with my dad. We both sweat lots more than anyone else we knew. By the time the song was over, Mr. Altman was smiling broadly.

"I'm blown away, Sloane. Your technique, your creativity and your concentration were really impressive." He walked over and put his arm around my shoulder. "Congratulations. The position of seventh grade dance captain is yours."

"Thank you, Mr. Altman. You won't be sorry," I gasped, still breathing hard. Molly and I already figured out the other two girls we'd ask to be on the dance team... Rebecca and Geena. Even though they were part of the official "mean girls" group at Lakeview Middle School, they were really good dancers. If we wanted to win, we'd have to suck it up and ignore their attitude. My mind fast-forwarded to the rehearsals that would fill the next few months.

Molly was waiting right outside the gym door. One look and she knew the news was good. We squealed, harmonizing with the bell signaling first period, then promised to continue the celebration at lunchtime.

The rest of the morning passed by in a blur. I couldn't wait to get to the cafeteria to tell my mother. One of the coolest things about middle school was the unwritten law entitling you to a cell phone. I noticed I missed a call from my father. Wow, he must be calling about my audition. I could picture him smiling when he found out the good news. Excitedly I pressed redial.

"Sloane?" my dad answered. Unconsciously, my hand gripped the receiver. There was something in his voice...not panic but the opposite, a flatness that made me nervous. He usually joked around whenever he called, disguising his voice to say he was Neil Efron or Neil Pattinson, whatever hot celeb came to mind. But not today. I felt my excitement going down the drain around my feet.

"What's wrong, dad?" I heard people talking in the background. "Where are you?"

"First, please don't worry. I hate to bother you at school but I'm at North Shore Hospital. The doctor didn't like the way my blood work came back. He thinks it might be some kind of blood disorder, I don't know."

His words rolled over me like a boulder, punching the air from my lungs. I tried taking comfort in the fact that he sounded more irritated than worried. My head began to pound.

"Listen, your mom just left here. I'm sure whatever this is, it'll be fine. But you know your mother…she's gets so emotional about these things. So I need your help. You're a calming influence on her. I'm thinking maybe you'd better head home right after school."

It seemed to me feeling emotional was totally appropriate. But I tried to match his tone. "Of course, Dad. How long do you think you'll be in the hospital?"

"It better not be long," he said testily. "You saw me this morning… I'm fine. That's why I'm calling so you could hear from me that everything's going to be OK. Just do me a favor and bring the garbage cans out to the curb and remind Mom to put on the outside lights before she goes to sleep."

Only my father. Lying in a hospital bed and his only concern was maintaining order at home. Mom would get mad when he'd bark commands at her so it was my job to assist him in running what he called a "tight ship." He'd remind me to turn on the sprinklers or change the cat's litter or make sure the alarm system was turned on. I kind of liked that he relied on me. He's called me his right hand man since I was four, before I had a clue what it meant. If it weren't for our efforts, he would say, we'd all drown by morning.

"Listen Sloane, honey, I gotta go. There's a pretty nurse here who wants to take my temperature. Remember…"

"The garbage and the lights…I remember," I said numbly.

"And check that the front door is locked," he said before hanging up.

A swarm of butterflies made a home in my stomach. I quickly gathered my things, feeling like I was about to take a test I didn't study for. How does a person get a blood disorder? How do you get rid of it?

I searched around the cafeteria, trying to find Molly. Although I was way across the room, her grin disappeared when she saw my face. She met me half way. I told her about my phone call. Her sympathetic hug lasted a long time. That scared me even more.

"Let's not talk about this anymore," I said, shaking my head as if to dislodge the grip my dad's news had on my brain. "We have a million things to decide about the dance."

We both glanced over to where Geena and Rebecca were sitting. The girls who sat at that table would say they were friends but they weren't the nutritious kind like Molly and me. They were all pretty good students, pretty good athletes, and I'll bet every one of them actually needed the bra they were wearing. Each nervously protected her seat at that table, knowing it stamped their ticket to popularity. When you were one of the half dozen or so allowed to have lunch there, it signified your membership in the tribe... the tribe of those who worship Geena.

If you called them the popular girls, they'd deny it, saying there was no such thing, that everybody is friends with everybody else... but you had to be popular to believe that. I guess I want to say they were just not as nice as the rest of us, but then it's so confusing. How can you be popular if most people don't like you?

"You have enough on your mind," sighed Molly. "They're both in my English class this afternoon. I'll flatter them into it... even though I think it's a mistake to have anything to do with them ever."

"They're not that bad," I said unconvincingly. "And we need the best dancers to win."

"Remember the week Geena wore those horrible tee shirts... *Better be late than to arrive ugly* and *I'm kind of a big deal?* Come on, you gagged too, admit it."

Molly was right, of course. But we didn't have a choice.

"Do you remember when Vanessa came to school with that silky pink shirt?" she went on.

Vanessa clung to her seat at that table like a lifeboat. Definitely the tag along, she barely hung on to her honored position. To insure her place, she cleaned up the table each day at the end of lunch period, filling her arms with everybody's garbage and walking across the cafeteria to throw it all way. She'd traded off being squished at the bottom of this totem pole for the chance to look popular to the rest of the grade.

"Yeah, I remember."

Ignoring my answer, Molly went on, determined to make her point.

'Well,' Geena said, 'you might like how you look in that shirt but you're mistaken.' Molly exhaled loudly. "I still picture poor Vanessa's face."

"Stop already. I get it. You don't like Geena. But it'll be fine, you'll see. No one wants to be center stage and come in first place more than those girls. And I'm not going to let her be the boss of me."

"OK, I'm not going to make your life miserable about it... especially not today. Just promise you'll keep on hating her as much as I do."

"Promise," I smiled.

After school I raced the six blocks to my house, barely paying attention to the two red lights on the way. When I got to the front door I used my keys rather than ring the bell as I usually would. It allowed me an extra second to sense the mood in the house before entering.

"Sloane, did you hear? Dad's in the hospital. He needs blood. His is infected. Mommy's taking me tomorrow to see if he could use my blood instead." Emma ran right into me, knocking my knapsack to the floor.

"Who told you that?" It was kind of sweet in a drama queen kind of way, that she was ready to save the day even if it involved needles and blood.

"Mommy. She's on the phone with the doctor right now. She said you'd give your blood later. He needs my blood first."

"Great, Emma, you're one brave little girl," I said, hanging my coat in the hall closet. I knew she couldn't possibly understand what was going on.

"Did you get to speak to Dad?"

"Uh-huh. He said he's not that sick. He just has to stay in the hospital till he gets my blood to help him."

I couldn't tell if she was purposely making up a story or just misunderstood the information she heard. Just then she heard the theme music of *Sam and Cat* and made her way back to the couch.

Thank God for TV, the best babysitter for the brain. She never noticed as I sneaked away to find my mother.

Mom was perched on the step stool in the kitchen, cradling the phone between her ear and her shoulder. Her back was toward me.

"I'll bring Emma in after school. Just tell me the truth…is the procedure painful? Will she feel dizzy or tired afterward?"

Mom's head sunk, turtle-like, between her shoulders as she listened to the doctor answer her questions.

"God, I wish I could be the donor." Her voice sounded about three octaves lower than usual, and raspy, like she'd been yelling and screaming for hours. She leaned against the wall and sighed.

More talk on the other end.

Then she said, "No, I'm praying the issue doesn't come up. Neil's having leukemia is enough to handle right now. That's why I asked if you'd be willing to test Sloane's blood anyway. It'll buy me some time before dealing with the other thing."

My face got hot. I quietly backed away from the kitchen doorway and ran into the bathroom and locked the door. I put down the toilet seat cover and sat down, my hands wrapped around my waist, bent over as if I had a bad stomachache. What to focus on first? Leukemia. People die from that. Pictures flashed before me. The shelf in the living room filled with racquetball trophies. How short he seemed last night.

Suddenly I realized I was sitting in the dark. I groped to find the light switch. Then I changed my mind. It was easier to focus without seeing. What was Mom talking about? Why would Emma, not me, donate first? Maybe it was our blood type. That A+, B-, universal donor stuff I didn't pay attention to in health class. But if that was all it was, what was "the other thing" she'd have to buy time to handle?

"Sloane, are you in there? Are you OK?" Mom was knocking on the bathroom door. I pushed the mysterious other thing out of my mind and got up to open the door.

We hugged in the dark without saying a word. For the first time in my life I felt my hug was doing for her what hers always did for me.

"When I spoke to Dad he wanted to make sure you don't forget to put on the outside lights tonight…"

Mom shook her head and held me tighter.

"I heard you say Dad has leukemia. On the phone he told me it was a blood disorder and made it seem like it was no big deal. But leukemia is a very big deal, right?"

My mother stiffened, as if I said something that made her afraid of me. It could only be she was terrified about what I overheard. Oh God. It *was* me; I was the issue she needed to "buy time" about. The room started spinning. If only I could rewind to an hour ago or fast forward to an hour from now… to be anywhere in time but here at this moment.

CHAPTER TWO

"When did you hear me say leukemia?" she said in a measured tone.

"When I walked in. You were on the phone with the doctor." Her stricken face forced me to continue.

"I heard the word leukemia and ran into the bathroom," I lied.

Her shoulders relaxed.

"He felt fine this morning. I don't understand."

"Me neither, honey," she sighed. "The doctor said some people have no symptoms at all." Mom shook her head. "After we eat and Emma goes to bed, I'll explain everything I know."

The two of us pretended to eat a slice of the pizza Mom bought on her way home from the hospital. It was a rare treat in our house — pizza for dinner. As Emma hummed, I envied her for being so young that a piece of pizza could make her feel better.

"How much blood are they going to take out of me? Like a gallon? Will they put me to sleep? Am I going to be in the same room as Daddy?"

Mom tried to be patient.

"Emma, they're just going to take a little bit of blood from you tomorrow. To see if your blood type matches Daddy's. If it does, then we'll know you can donate some more if one day he needs a bone marrow transplant."

Emma inhaled, about to begin the next litany of questions, but Mom cut her short.

"We're all going to have to take this one day at a time. The first step is finding out for sure whether Dad has leukemia. Then, if he does, they'll have to see what kind." Her eyes filled. "He's probably going to be in the hospital for a while."

She grabbed one of my hands and one of Emma's.

"We are all going to do whatever we have to do to help make Daddy well."

The three of us just sat there for what seemed like an hour, like we were at a séance or something. Then abruptly Mom said, "OK, Emma, get ready for bed. I want to talk to Sloane for a few minutes."

Usually telling Emma to go to bed signals the start of a series of negotiations. I'm not tired yet. You forgot to test me on my spelling words. Can I stay down five more minutes? But tonight she got right up and headed for the stairs.

"Come up and kiss me good night. Both of you." She never asked me to kiss her goodnight.

"Sure. We'll be right up," I said quietly.

Mom smiled gratefully. She got up from the table and took the phone off the hook.

"I don't want to be interrupted."

I couldn't decide if her undivided attention was more flattering or frightening.

"Dr. Ruden suspects Dad has acute leukemia," she began, folding the pizza box in half to make it fit in the garbage. "They've already started him on antibiotics. Tonight they're going to give him a transfusion to replace some red blood cells."

"There's a possibility it's not leukemia, right?" I asked.

Mom nodded. "But they don't seem too hopeful." She closed her eyes and took a deep breath. Then she opened them and looked straight at me.

"I'm not going to lie to you, Sloane. This is not going away for a long time. Dad will probably be starting chemotherapy in a few days. He's going to feel lousy for a while before he feels better."

"So why is Emma saying Dad needs her blood, not mine?"

Again Mom looked startled, like I caught her going through my drawers or something. I continued to stare into her eyes. She looked away first.

"Why Emma's blood?" I repeated. "I'm older than she is."

Mom's face dissolved. She put her hands over her eyes and started to rock back and forth. I felt nauseous.

"It's all too much. Too much," she sobbed.

At that instant, I understood what the expression "fear of the unknown," meant. This must be the other thing Mom had been talking about.

"Mom, please talk to me."

God, why did I listen to her conversation, why did I ask about Emma. My mind was racing. I couldn't imagine what could upset her more than the news Dad had leukemia.

"All right, Sloane," Mom began slowly. "I'm going to explain why Emma's blood is being tested before yours."

I was breathing fast, my body already reacting to news I hadn't yet heard.

"What I'm going to share with you, no one else in the world knows. Not even Grandma and Grandpa." She swallowed hard.

Ordinarily, I love secrets but I knew this one would be terrifyingly different.

"When your father and I decided to start a family, we learned Dad's sperm count was too low for me to become pregnant." She paused to blow her nose in her napkin.

Mom never, ever, did that. "All we cared about was having a baby. We decided the most reasonable solution was to borrow sperm from a sperm bank." She scanned my face. "Do you understand what I'm saying?"

I didn't. Oh, how I wished I paid more attention in fifth grade when all this egg and sperm stuff was explained. I had seen photos of Mom pregnant with me. Dad even took pictures in the delivery room when I was born, revealing way more than I was comfortable knowing. Sort of like this conversation.

"What, you're not my real parents? I don't get it."

"Of course we're your real parents," Mom said. Her lips formed a smile but there was no happiness behind it. "It's just that…"

"Dad's not my biological father," I whispered in astonishment. The news felt like a rush of clean white snow coming at me in an avalanche.

She nodded. "Are you all right?" she said anxiously.

Was I all right? I shook my head. How could a person answer a question like that? Sure. My father's in the hospital with a life-threatening disease, but not to worry. He's not really my dad, after all.

We sat there in silence, listening to the ticking of the kitchen clock. Funny how loud quiet can feel.

"Sloane, did you make dance captain? I forgot to ask you," yelled down Emma.

"Yes, Emma, I did," I shouted back. "I'll show you the new combination I'm working on tomorrow."

Mom glanced upstairs. "I'm sorry, Sloane. That's wonderful news." Again she tried to smile.

I shrugged. Had that happened this morning?

"Go on," I persisted, "why didn't you ever tell me about this?"

"At the time we were both counseled it was better for everyone involved never to share that we used donor insemination. And Dad and I agreed it was nobody's business."

Not even mine? I thought dully. Maybe especially not mine. Then it hit me. "What about Emma?" I blurted out. "How come you didn't have to borrow sperm to make her?"

Mom sighed. "We don't know. After four years, I suddenly became pregnant. It was a miracle."

I flinched. Emma was a miracle. Emma was their child.

"Come on up, you guys. You promised you'd kiss me good night."

Mom dabbed her eyes. "Oh Sloane, believe me, talking to you about this…under these conditions…is the hardest thing I've ever had to do. Don't be mad. I couldn't bear it right now."

Mad? Was I mad? Maybe, but that was way down the list after devastated, confused, worried and numb.

"Can we talk about this tomorrow?" I said, suddenly exhausted.

"Of course, darling," Mom said, relieved. "There's not much more I can tell you but you can ask me anything."

Later that night, I lay in bed, wondering if Dad was sleeping. This had to be, without a doubt, the worst day in both our lives. Our worlds were changed forever, no matter what happened next.

As I turned to shut off the light, I wondered if he was sweating too.

CHAPTER THREE

The good news was that Emma was a match. She'd be able to supply her bone marrow if my father needed a transplant. The bad news was that never before did I feel so alone. I was too empty inside to cry. I didn't want to face my dad. And I felt guilty asking Mom any more questions. My reaction was not at all what I would have expected, given the kind of person I was. But maybe, I reasoned, that was because I wasn't that person after all. Who was I? How could someone who doesn't know where half of her came from, begin to answer such a question.

Mom explained they "borrowed" some sperm to help her conceive. Now I felt like I was borrowing someone else's family. It was mind boggling. Grandma and Grandpa weren't even related to me. Emma was my half sister. Dad was...I don't know what Dad was.

I started thinking of how it all made sense. Not that he wasn't proud when I got good grades, but it didn't compare to how much he *loved* when Emma won a swimming match. My father wasn't the only dad to fall asleep during the long dance recitals I put him through, but he was the only dad who stood up and whistled at Emma's soccer games. Now I understood why he and Emma laughed when the bug zapper would hiss in our backyard each summer, claiming another victim and I never got the joke. They were among the zappers in life. I was a zapee.

Not that he showed it, but how disappointed he must have been when I turned out to enjoy ballet more than softball, and reading more than jumping on the trampoline he bought for me. Till Emma came along to make things right. Who could blame him for preferring his own flesh and blood, a daughter who clearly inherited his abilities, over me?

Here was the man who, when I was six, made me go back and return a pack of Bazooka bubble gum I'd taken from the drug store. Cheating and lying, he carefully explained as I returned the stolen property to the cashier, were among the worse things a person could do. In spite of how much harder being honest appears at the moment, he'd said, in the long run telling the truth was always easier.

Obviously not always.

"Most couples who use artificial insemination to create their families don't tell their children," my mother said three nights later, the first opportunity we had to continue our conversation. "They feel, what's the point?"

Seriously? The point was huge. It was hard to believe that she couldn't understand letting a child know she was created using a stranger's sperm is important information for her to have.

Poor Mom looked drained but I couldn't stop asking questions. "Why the big secret? Were you guys ashamed? Embarrassed?"

"Of course not," she responded too quickly. She fidgeted with the top button on her blouse. "Look, Sloane, I am beyond sorry you had to find out this way. You have a right to be upset, but please let's not discuss this with anyone just yet. There will be time later on, I promise, when Dad gets well, to talk about it all you want. For the next few weeks, our priority has to be getting him back home."

She paused.

"We have to protect him from any unnecessary stress now," she said with a catch in her voice.

Of course she was right. It was selfish of me to be so impatient. I would have to wait.

That night felt a month long. Disjointed images jerked me awake a dozen times.

My mind raced crazily from the family tree I researched so carefully in fifth grade, hanging in the basement, now half a lie, to when I was five and saw my father fall to his knees and cry when I ran into the street and barely escaped getting hit by a car. I turned on the light and stared at the ceiling, trying to slow down my heart.

How awful it must have been for him to find out he couldn't have a child of his own. I wonder how long it took him to get used to raising a baby like me... and how often he still thought about it. Although this information could have, maybe should have, made him seem even more special to me, it didn't. I shook my head to stop the thoughts from coming. Ugh, this wasn't helping sleep come any quicker.

I turned on the bathroom light and looked in the mirror. On my family tree, I said my ancestors came from Russia and Poland. But this girl in the reflection, where were her great-grandparents from? Where did she get those deep blue eyes? Her parents and Emma had brown eyes. And her height? By next year I will certainly be the tallest one in the family photos.

My poor, scared mom, all she wanted was to protect me from what I was feeling now... an identity splintered. I knew she needed me to comfort her and tell her I was OK. But I didn't feel OK. I understood that I was loved, so why was I feeling so lost? Because I always believed I had my grandmother's tiny ear lobes and my Aunt Carrie's long fingers? No. It was because if genetics didn't matter, they could just hand out babies at random in the maternity ward.

I wasn't interested in finding a new daddy. My dad is my dad. But I still needed to know where I came from. And not feel like a terrible person for admitting it.

The middle school cafeteria smelled of French fries and damp sweaters. As always during lunch period, it was crowded and loud.

"So Sloane, I changed my mind," Molly began, "I think I'm going to own a labradoodle, instead of a golden retriever."

This must be the fifth time she changed her mind. No one but me knew she meant when she graduated from college and we lived together in New York City. We rarely needed to mention when or where something was going to happen. Our silent conversations were a habit that came with being best friends since first grade. Whether we

talked about our soon-to-appear breasts or our probably never-going –
to-happen boyfriends, it was clear we were not only on the same page,
we occupied the same sentence.

People even said we looked alike, with our dark curly hair,
sprinkling of freckles and blue eyes. Molly had braces. She wanted me
to get them too but I kind of liked the gap between my two front
teeth. I was a little taller; she had a dimple. And we both chose to wear
our sweats in a medium rather than a small, not because the small
didn't fit, but because the mediums were more comfortable.

Molly gulped her cranberry juice. This was our second week of
drinking cranberry juice in little glass bottles with our lunch. We were
the only ones in our class who did and it was Molly's idea to see if we
could start a trend. Not that too many of the things we liked ever made
it to anybody else's top ten list. We enjoyed the retro black and white
shows on TV Land more than we liked *Pretty Little Liars*. We both
hung horoscope calendars in our bedrooms and believed there was
definitely something awesome about how often they were right. And
we knew it was just a matter of time till our dance videos went viral on
Utube.

It had been four days since I heard the biggest secret of all time. If
I didn't tell someone that half of me came from an aluminum test tube
immersed for God knows how long in God knows what, I would
explode. I had to trust Molly, I had to. I sat up straight and squared my
shoulders.

"Oh Sloane," said Molly, interrupting my thoughts, "I'm so sorry.
I'm going on and on when you must be obsessed with what's going on
with your father."

"Well, yes I am," I said, speaking very slowly, "but he's not the man
you know in the hospital."

Bingo. She put down her cranberry juice.

"I just found out there's another guy somewhere out there who is
actually my biological father. And I don't have a clue who he is."

For the first time in recorded history, Molly was speechless. I
explained all I knew, repeating what my mother told me. I said that
because my dad had some problem called a low sperm count, he and
my mother went to a doctor who recommended a sperm bank. There

they both picked out a donor, some man who had the same color hair as my dad. Then they borrowed, as my mother so delicately put it, his sperm to make me.

"No way," I heard her exhale.

"And they never ever had any intention of telling me. If my father didn't get sick and I didn't overhear my mom on the phone, I still wouldn't know. By the way, my mother made me promise not to tell anyone but I had to tell you."

"Jeez, Sloane, this is insane. You must be freaking out."

"I am."

The loudness of my voice surprised me. Suddenly I felt a force like a tornado building up inside of me.

"All those years of playing soccer and hating it, always feeling I was disappointing my dad because I sucked no matter where the coach put me." My heart was beating fast. "It's not fair."

Then Molly asked the million dollar question. "What about Emma? Was she made out of the same sperm as you were?"

"No," I snickered, "she's actually my parents' real child. She's one hundred percent natural. No frozen, artificial ingredients. A miracle, my mother called her." I felt the muscle in my jaw twitching and wondered if Molly could see it.

She just stared into my eyes and said quietly, "Is that what's bothering you most … that Emma is your father's child?"

I didn't answer.

"If you're thinking what I think you're thinking, you're wrong," Molly said gently. "Your father is an award winning football coach. He pushes everyone that way, not just you."

When I didn't reply, she went on. "Living together for your whole life makes someone a parent, not some squiggly sperm guys. You have to know your parents love you as much as they love Emma."

My stomach tightened. Molly meant well but she couldn't possibly understand.

"I'm not saying my parents don't care about me, but finding out something like this and then being expected to forget it, it's not fair." I swallowed hard. "Maybe this donor guy, whoever he is, loves the beach like I do. Maybe he hated Spanish when he was in middle school because he was also terrible at languages. You know how you make fun of how sometimes when I laugh, I snort? Or when I sneeze, I always sneeze three times? Maybe that's from him. My biological father."

Molly didn't answer right away. Then she said, "I feel bad for you Sloane, I really do. I can't even imagine…. But Neil Davis is your dad, not some fantasy guy who handed down his cute sneezes and snorts."

It was a mistake to tell Molly. She obviously thought I was an awful daughter to even think about this guy now. But I couldn't help it. I wasn't stupid enough to think he was perfect… I just had to find out who he was. What he looked like. Whether he'd be more impressed with a 94 in social studies than how fast I could run.

I didn't have a clue how you go about tracing a phantom sperm donor from almost thirteen years ago but I agreed with my mother. This wasn't anyone else's business but mine.

CHAPTER FOUR

The hospital was only five blocks away from the middle school. At first I was happy to be able to walk over and see my dad on my own. That quickly became a mixed blessing.

"It's four o'clock. Isn't it time for my medication?" he'd yell into the intercom attached to the nurses' station at two minutes after four. "Tell the doctor these vegetables have all the nutrients nuked out of them," he'd growl to the aide who brought his dinner. "You look a little pale. Are you sure this job isn't too much for you?" he'd question a frightened young Candy Striper when she'd deliver his mail. He treated his diagnosis of leukemia like it was the visiting team. And he treated the hospital staff like he was their coach .

The doctors were another story. His mission was to impress them with how quickly he'd recover from each bout of chemotherapy. Mouth sores, pneumonia, fevers. They invaded, he conquered.

"When can I get out of here?" he asked everyone who walked into his room. "I've got a life to live, you know."

Dr. Ruden knew how to handle him. "I wish all my patients had your spirit, Neil. No doubt you'll break the record for the quickest bounce back in North Shore's history."

Everyone played games in that room. Mom babbled on about who was voted off *The Voice*. Dad made believe he was still in control of everyone and everything. And I, the biggest actor of them all, made believe nothing had changed.

Mostly I followed instructions, same as always. Dad never noticed anything different about my behavior. He asked how I was doing in school, I told him great. If he wanted to know how the talent show was going, I told him terrific. Only when Emma's name came up did he really listen. She was too young to be allowed up to visit him and he missed her terribly.

"Why don't you head out, sweetheart?" he'd say to me after a half hour. "Emma's home alone."

She was usually at a friend's house but I'd just get up and leave.

"Sure, Dad. I'll give her your love."

"Good. See you tomorrow. Don't forget to lower the thermostat when you go to bed. I don't even want to see those heating bills when I get home."

Each day was heavy with the weight of some shadowy unnamed thing sitting on my chest as soon as I opened my eyes in the morning. As time dribbled on, I lugged it around all day. And the next. And the next. My life felt like a never-ending January Monday. Only the twice a week dance rehearsals kept me going.

"Hey, how's your dad feeling?" Mr. Altman asked one afternoon.

"He's getting there," I answered. That was one of my three automatic responses when people asked. I rotated it with, "He's hanging in," and, regardless of whether it was true, "He's getting a little stronger every day."

"Look, for whatever it's worth, I think you're doing a great job of taking care of business. You work hard. And your focus is inspiring to the rest of the girls."

His words felt like a warm bath. I wanted to confess that I felt like a duck paddling furiously underneath the surface of the water. No matter how much I worried about my father's illness, I still found time to obsess about the insemination thing. Both issues just wore out my brain.

So I concentrated on the dance. My worries burned off as soon as the music started. I closed my eyes. Slamming down a move demanded the highest mental and physical imagination. Everything becomes clear as you push fast forward on adrenaline. On stage, I was free and fearless. In charge in a way I never was in the rest of my life. No one knew those moments were my only refuge, where gratefully there was no chance to think.

It was hard to believe that lemony vanilla Geena and citrusy cinnamon Rebecca were taking orders from me.

"I love what you did there!" exclaimed Geena after I demonstrated the next combination. "It's like old school Britney plus classic Beyonce. Totally rad."

"Thanks," I smiled, a little embarrassed how much her compliment meant to me. I could smell her mango lip gloss from across the stage.

"Have you ever danced to gangsta rap?"

"Nah," I said, "I like some of the lyrics but the beat isn't enough for me. I've given up trying to choreograph leaps and kicks to it."

"I totally agree," Geena grinned. Then she walked over to where I was standing. "I hope you don't take this the wrong way," she whispered, "but if you bought those sweats in a smaller size, they'd look so much better."

I looked down at my comfortable baggy pants…then at her yoga pants rolled down to her hips.

"And that tee shirt? It's cute with jeans but if you cut off the neck, rolled up the sleeves and wore a beater underneath…" she let the sentence hang in the air.

My face was hot. I glanced over at Molly in her oversized sweats, then back at Geena. I couldn't ignore that she knew what she was talking about.

"Look," Geena said, "I like you. I like that you're smart and you have self confidence. Then she looked right into my eyes and said, "There are only a few of us, you know. We should really stick together."

A few of us? Us, meaning her and me?

"I know you don't like me very much…but we could really help each other. It's hard to find someone else who couldn't care less who disagrees with her." Then she leaned over and kissed me on the cheek.

"Just promise you'll think it over, that maybe you might be wrong about me."

Out of the corner of my eye I saw Molly staring at us. She bit her lip and looked away, just in time to miss me returning Geena's hug.

"Do you think Mommy will have time to get us presents for Chanukah?" Emma asked the next day.

Their child's cute little voice irritated me. Words from the dark side tumbled out without a censor.

"Is that all you think about? Dad's lying there, moaning and groaning, and all you care about is your Chanukah gifts? Unbelievable." I even shook my head for effect. "Like that's all that's on Mom's mind."

I was getting plates out of the cabinet. I knew Mom already shopped for the holiday, but suddenly being mean to Emma was like scratching an itch. It felt good.

"No," Emma said guiltily, "that's not all I think about. I was just wondering, that's all." She sat down at the table. "Does Daddy really moan and groan? Whenever I call him he sounds regular and he keeps saying he's getting better." She paused. "He is getting better, isn't he?"

She looked really small sitting there. Their miracle.

"Why do you ask? Because if he gets worse you get the chance to save his life with your magic blood?" Bulls-eye.

Emma's face got red. "You're such a jerk. Why are you acting so mean to me?" Her lower lip started to quiver. "I'm sorry if I was being selfish. If Daddy comes home, I don't need any presents. Is that better?"

"Look," I said, bringing a pitcher of iced tea to the table, "you can say whatever you want. You don't have to act cutesy for me. I'm not Dad."

"You're a horrible sister, Sloane, to say that." Emma faltered. "No wonder Dad wants my blood and not yours. Yours is creepy."

She got up from the table and ran out of the kitchen.

I heard her door slam upstairs. Calmly I took out my cheeseburger and fries and opened the newspaper to the comics. They said letting pent up emotions spill out was supposed to make you feel better. I went to get a napkin and saw my reflection in the toaster oven. Obviously when it comes to me, that was not the case.

I started cutting back on my visits to the hospital. The constant bombardment of chemotherapy was taking its toll. Sometimes when I walked into the room, dad's face would be turned toward the window and he wouldn't even acknowledge me.

He was uncomfortable with anyone seeing him so weak and vulnerable. And he had a thing about pain killers and tranquilizers and sleeping pills…they were only for people who couldn't take it… weaklings who needed a crutch. He had to stay clear and sharp. That way he could still be the boss of everyone.

"What about that anti-nausea medicine?" I asked after one particularly tough bout of throwing up. It was painful to witness his stubbornness. "Is it against your religion to take something guaranteed to make you feel better?"

"That pill dopes me up. It puts me in a fog, all fuzzy and woozy for hours. I hate that, feeling outside of myself."

Outside of myself is exactly where I'd want to be if I were him. It was where I'd rather be, being me. My grandma had a friend who had two children. One died of cancer, the other in a car accident, both in their 20s. In my neighborhood there's a house that got hit by lightning one summer and had to be completely rebuilt. The next year, a hurricane ripped a hundred-fifty-year-old oak tree from their front lawn and sent it smashing through the brand new roof. In both cases it seemed God made a mistake. That He went too heavy on the helping of bad luck. My grandfather always said you never got more heartache than God thought you could handle. I was pretty sure my grandfather was wrong.

CHAPTER FIVE

With Dad out of the house, the mood was dark but quiet. The three of us fell into a monotonous, yet strangely comforting, routine. After weeks of trudging through the same exhausting schedule you couldn't really focus on how awful what was happening really was. Then after a month in the hospital, Dad came home. Silence was replaced by chaos. Our house overflowed with visitors and pills and makeshift comfort stations everywhere…and Grandma and Grandpa.

As soon as Dad came home, they flew in from Florida to help take care of their son. Having them around sounded kind of nice at first, but after a few days reality set in. Live-in Boca Raton early-bird-dinner-eaters belonged in their natural habitat, not under our roof on Long Island.

They'd moved to Florida three years ago when Grandpa retired from his job as the general manager of a paint and wallpaper store. We all worried how he'd adjust after forty years of seventy-hour weeks, standing on his feet behind the counter. He had no hobbies and few friends. But he surprised us. In no time he took up golf, was elected to the condominium's Board of Directors and was ripping out coupons for two-for-one dinners like a pro.

Grandma, on the other hand, with her orangey pixie haircut and huge red framed glasses, had been Florida material for years. Decked out in her pastel warm-up suits — always either jeweled or fringed or splashed with metallic paint — she was warmly welcomed at Sunrise Towers. She even had the prerequisite calling card hanging from her neck: a gold chain strung with gold charms engraved with the faces of all her children and grandchildren.

Emma was in heaven. She was so busy cuddling on Dad's lap, having Gram make her Rice Krispy Treats, and talking Grandpa into testing her on her spelling words, she never noticed that days went by without me saying a word to her.

Dad walked around the house in sweats that suddenly were way too big and a baseball cap to hide whatever hair he had left. Soon I realized it might be months before we'd be able to discuss what I'd found out.

Grandma spent her days recreating the foods Dad loved as a child. She was a woman on a mission. Her son had to eat and she'd make him — or kill herself in the kitchen trying. Our whole house smelled like it was 1969. She started slow with Wheatina, Ovaltine and Jello with bananas. Then she pulled out the big guns — fried chicken cutlets, meatloaf and mashed potatoes, coconut custard pie.

"Leave him alone, Carol," Grandpa would say gently, as she'd try everything short of putting the fork in his mouth to make him eat. "If he's not hungry, he's not hungry."

But she was my father's mother, the source of his headstrong nature. "I know," she'd answer, "I know. But this is all I can do to help him. So it has to work."

It was hard for them to see their son so frail. "Ach, this is not right. It's not natural," I overheard Grandpa say. "We should be the sick ones, not him."

Grandma sighed. "When is leukemia natural? When is it right?"

Social chit-chat was never Dad's game. He hated being unable to control who walked in or how long they'd stay. As visitors left, he'd yell out, "I appreciate you took the time to stop by, but please don't feel you have to do it again."

Mom cringed.

"I can't take that look of pity in their eyes, Karen," he would say, "Just tell everyone the doctor said no visitors."

He never noticed that sometimes Mom enjoyed the company. Or that new faces distracted all of us from thinking about what lie ahead.

I walked around feeling like a neglected plant, badly in need of sunlight and water.

"What's wrong, lovey?" Gram asked one night after dinner. "Your grandfather and I don't like how you've been acting lately."

The three of us were the only ones left at the table.

"Right, Al?" she asked, raising her eyebrows and nodding her head as a signal for him to continue.

Grandpa cleared his throat. He always did before saying something he had thought about for a long time. "Your grandmother and I were talking. We understand these are hard times for you, Sloane, but your father is going to make it. We know he's going to recover from this."

I didn't respond.

"You haven't smiled in days," my grandma noted. "I see something is weighing heavy on my angel's heart. Your poor mother is too worried about your father to notice, but we know something's bothering you. Grandpa thinks it's just the leukemia. I'm not so sure."

My eyes filled with tears when she called me her angel. My grandfather came over and put my face between his two huge hands.

"If your parents can't help you right now, maybe we can. Haven't you heard how wise we old people are? That's because there's not much we haven't heard before. Talk to us, Sloane. Please."

I laid my cheek in one of his hands and closed my eyes. Here was my sunlight.

"I doubt you'll be able to help with this," I said carefully. "It might be the one thing you've never heard before."

"What could be so bad?" my grandmother said dismissively, taking the seat next to me. She motioned for Grandpa to move over to the chair on my other side. Then she pushed the hair out of my eyes. "You are just as important to us as anyone else in this house. And nothing could ever make us love you any less."

I took a deep breath.

"Even if I told you that you weren't actually my grandparents?"

They looked at each other.

"This I don't understand," Gram said in bewilderment. "Is this some slang expression from the Internet?"

"Shhhh," said Grandpa, putting his finger to his lips. "Explain what you mean, Sloane, that we're not your grandparents. Did you disown us when we weren't looking?" He tried to joke but his eyes were serious.

"Mom told me not to tell anybody. But I can't take it anymore. If I tell you, do you promise not to say anything to her?"

They both stared at me and nodded. I told them about the conversation I overheard between my mother and the doctor. And the talk Mom and I had afterward. And the miracle of Emma.

"Low sperm count?" Grandpa said wonderingly. "Carol, did Neil ever say anything to you about a low sperm count?"

"Me he should talk to about sperm? He'd discuss such things with you, never me." She put her hand on her forehead, as if all of a sudden her head was too heavy for her neck to support.

"It did take a few years before Karen got pregnant, remember? She went to a special doctor for tests and she told us she was fine…It never entered my mind Neil was the reason she was having problems. Al, do you believe this?"

"If Sloane is telling me, of course I believe it." He turned to me. "So what you're saying," said Grandpa slowly, trying to absorb it all, "is that Neil, uh, Dad, didn't really give you his own, uh, genes. That uh, someone we don't know gave you his DNA, is that right?"

"So now what, we're strangers? DNA, ZNA, what's the difference? We're a family," said Gram, quickly regaining her composure. "You're our granddaughter. End of story."

She glanced over at Grandpa to back her up. But he didn't notice. He was staring at me.

"Sloane looks just like your brother's granddaughter, Amy, from Cincinnati. Remember, Al, we saw her a few years ago at the wedding?" Grandpa didn't answer.

"Didn't we come home and tell you that you have a twin in Cincinnati?" Gram demanded.

"Boy, oh boy," Grandpa muttered, dropping his eyes. "This kind of news must be very hard on you."

I shook my head yes.

"You weren't worried we would feel differently about you, were you?" he asked, his voice shaking a little.

"No," I said smiling feebly. "If I was afraid of that, I never could've told you. It's just that…"

"Well, you got that right," interrupted Grandma. "I mean, I know you don't find out something like this every day, but although it's shocking, crazy even, the good part is nothing's changed." The certainty in her voice pleased her. "Even if you aren't Neil's real...I don't mean real...Al, what do I mean?"

"Biological. Neil's biological daughter." Grandpa looked embarrassed.

"Right," Grandma said emphatically. "Even though you're not his flesh and blood, you're still our Sloane, the granddaughter we love."

She actually sounded proud that she was big-hearted enough not to instantly stop caring about me.

"Go on, Sloane," Grandpa said, catching my eye and holding it just long enough to let me know he realized there was more I wanted to say.

I looked at each of them, my heart thumping. "I don't know how to explain that even though you're both handling this amazingly well, I'm not. Don't get me wrong, I'm grateful you both still love me. I don't know what I'd do if you didn't. But this can't be end of story for me."

Once again they exchanged looks.

"Did you ever hear the expression, 'let sleeping dogs lie'?" Gram asked. She sounded calm but she sat up extremely straight in her chair.

"And that means..." I shot back, trying unsuccessfully to keep an edge out of my voice.

"It means," answered Gram, ignoring my tone, "that why tell the world your father had a low sperm count thirteen years ago. In the scheme of things..."

"In the scheme of things," I broke in, "normal children are connected to their parents by hundreds of things they inherit from them. Human beings are not like flowers. They don't go around spreading their pollen and sending their seeds into the wind." My voice rose. "It makes a difference to me whose sperm made me. Even if it doesn't, to anyone else in the world."

I got up from the table.

"Look, you two are the best," I said, directing my words to Grandpa. "I'm not mad at you. It would just be nice if someone could try to see this through my eyes."

Neither of them said a word. For the first time, my grandfather looked away.

"Maybe another time we'll talk some more," I finished, my voice dropping off self consciously.

My grandmother's voice hardened. "As far as I'm concerned, more talk, more trouble." She paused. "I don't want to discuss this ever again," she half whispered, her lower lip trembling. "My son's upstairs fighting for his life. If he found out we knew about this, it would make him feel terrible." She folded her arms across her chest. "I'm sorry, Sloane, but I'm going to make believe we never had this discussion."

My grandfather remained silent. He looked uncomfortable, but this was a blood-is-thicker-than-water matter and he obviously decided to let Gram be the bad guy.

"You have a long life ahead to work out any problems this gene mix-up thing is causing you," she went on. "We owe it to your father to respect his privacy." She looked down and closed her eyes. Then, a few seconds later, she looked up and smiled.

It was bizarre, as if she literally shook the information out of her consciousness.

"Anyone for ice cream?" she asked brightly.

CHAPTER SIX

"OK, so we'll meet back here on Wednesday to start marking the dance," I announced. "I'm going to break up our three minute routine into ten thirty second combinations. We won't start the next one till we all feel good about the one we've been practicing. Is that all right?"

"I thought hip hop was more free style," Geena declared. "And that we'd all be making up our dance together."

What I wanted to say was that you thought wrong. Instead I said, "Hip hop is just as structured as jazz or modern dance. There are real positions just like releve and plie in ballet... because they all don't have French names doesn't mean they're not just as precise." My voice grew stronger. "Each step you make has to line up with everyone else's. I've worked really hard to put together some amazing moves..."

"Well, I made up some pretty great steps too," Geena interjected, raising her chin. "Can't we vote on the ones we like best?"

I felt Molly squeezing my arm.

She really wasn't being unreasonable. I just didn't want to deal. It wasn't her fault her table with their multi-colored beads around their necks and the dozen slim shiny bangles on their wrists, all coordinated with the layering... tank top under tee shirt under short zip up hoodie... always made me feel that if one of those *VH 1* fashion patrols came along, I'd be the yuck at the end of the yeah, yeah, yeahs.

"Why don't you wait to see what I've come up with first?" I asked, looking directly into Geena's ridiculously green eyes.

"That's fair," she answered with a big grin. In that instant I realized she was testing me…and by standing up to her, I had passed. Once again, it bothered me just a little how good that made me feel.

Then she bent down to pick up an empty wrapper from a small bag of spicy Doritos Molly and I shared.

"Now that we're officially in training, should you really be eating chips?" she asked Molly, her melon glossed lips parting in a big smile.

"Should you really care what I'm eating?" Molly answered in the most intimidating voice she could muster.

My stomach tightened.

"Don't be that way. I'm just trying to help." She dismissed Molly and turned her attention back to me.

"And I'm here to help you too. No one in this school knows more about hip hop … or hates not coming in first more than me. Remember that."

I nodded, wondering what it feels like to look like that, smell like that and be so sure of your every word. To be admired and to be disliked for being that admired. And not seem to care about any of it.

"So what's going on at home?" Molly asked when we spoke that night. "Not that the fact your skin is the color of Elmer's Glue gives me any clue."

"I hate my life," I sighed. "As my grandmother would say, end of story."

"Which part is the hardest? Worrying about your dad being sick? Dealing with your grandparents moving in?"

I had to trust her with the truth.

"I can't stop fixating about the man somewhere out there… and every time I think about him, I feel disgusting, like I'm the world's worst daughter."

If I expected sympathy for being so honest, I was mistaken.

"Come on, Sloane." She sounded annoyed.

My jaw clenched. "You're not fair, Molly. It's not like I'm thinking he's rich or an astronaut or he lives in Europe. It's the not knowing … and that just doesn't go away."

"And I hope you're getting over the Emma thing," she went on, ignoring what I said. "None of this is her fault, you know. Zachary told me how worried she was in school the other day that your father wasn't getting any better."

Molly's brother was in Emma's class. Why was everything coming out of Molly's mouth so insanely annoying? That never happened.

Then she said something and I understood.

"And what's with you and your new bff, Geena? All huggy and kissy face?"

"What are you talking about? Didn't you hear me answer her today? She tried to take over and I wouldn't let her." I paused. "I thought you'd be proud of me instead of acting jealous."

"Jealous? I'm not jealous of Geena, she's horrible. You heard her today about the Doritos wrapper," Molly said. "You better never let her see that you eat a sandwich at lunch. That would mean you are not on a diet. And if you're not on a diet, that means you're not obsessed with how you look. With those girls, if you don't think you're fat, you're conceited. And there's nothing worse you can be … not a tomboy or geeky or smelly… than a girl who feels OK about the way she looks in the mirror."

"Please, just listen to yourself. Can't you stop hating her till after the talent show?"

Molly took a deep breath. "I don't hate anyone… but I do hate the idea that you're defending her."

I laughed uneasily. The rest of our conversation was friendly enough, but careful. I knew it was the best we could hope for that night.

That night after everyone was asleep, I went back downstairs. I quietly opened the closet in the den, took out my baby album, and brought it back up to my room. I sat cross-legged on the floor, searching for some bit of information that might lead to the next step on my journey. Unfortunately, all my mother clipped, pasted and wrote about started the day I was born, not nine months before.

Mom kept a meticulously detailed diary of my first year and recorded every height and weight change, every burp, and every new habit with an exclamation point. Seven pounds, two ounces! Begin rice cereal! Sloane stands! The first page listed what was happening in the world the year I was born. The US space shuttle Columbia crashes. The United States launches war on Iraq. A blackout hits the U.S., Canada and Britain. What did I expect to find? A photo of a test tube? A withdrawal slip from a sperm bank? One of Mom's thank you notes, neatly mentioning how grateful she and Dad were for Mr. X's contribution?

I turned the pages. There was my birth certificate. Mother: Karen Gelb, age 26. Father: Neil Davis, age 28. The thought occurred to me that Davis wasn't even my real last name. I let that simple fact sink in. I wondered if I was really Irish...or Italian...or German. Grandma would love that.

Pages of congratulatory cards followed. Then a pediatrician's appointment card for six weeks after I was born. Suddenly I noticed that underneath it, on the same page, was another appointment card, this one for Mom. One thirty, May 30th, six-week check up for Karen Davis. Dr. Henry Prince, gynecologist. My heart started to beat quicker. He must be the doctor who delivered me, who took care of Mom throughout her pregnancy. Dear old Henry had to have known about the insemination.

I got up from the floor to get a piece of paper to copy down his telephone number. Suddenly there was a knock on my door. It was almost midnight.

"Can I come in?" whispered my dad's voice.

To say this was highly unusual would be an understatement. I couldn't remember the last time my father had been in my room. Probably last summer when he replaced the storm windows with screens.

"Uh, sure Dad. Just a second." I shoved the open album under my bed. Quickly I opened my history book to a page at random and put it face down on my bed. Then I opened the door.

"Are you OK? What are you doing up?" I asked, noticing what a skinny, shadowy figure he made standing there in the hallway.

"I have to take this medication every night at 12 o'clock," he said as he walked past me, into my room. He held up a plastic bottle. "Every six hours."

"Oh," I said, pretending this was fascinating news. I glanced nervously around the room, following his eyes. He squinted at the photos of my favorite groups wedged around my mirror.

"Got any from Prospect Park?" he asked wryly.

"The group's name is Linkin Park, Dad." I said, gladdened at his feeble attempt at humor. "Why do you ask?"

I pretended not to notice the grimace on his face as he lowered himself slowly into my desk chair.

"I ask because I'm trying to start a conversation. You and I haven't said more than a few words in weeks. I knew more about what was going on in your life when I was in the hospital."

I shrugged, forcing myself to look into his watery eyes. It made me realize how long it had been since we made eye contact. Obviously neither of us was comfortable revealing what might be discovered behind a closer look.

"I was on my way to the bathroom when I saw your light was still on. What's the matter, can't sleep?"

"Oh, I can sleep," I said pretending to yawn. "We have a quiz in American history tomorrow and I'm just going over the reading." My palms were sweating.

"What are you up to?" he asked, leaning toward my bed and picking up the textbook.

We were discussing Reconstruction, the period right after the Civil War. But I had no idea what page Dad was looking at right now.

"Still on the War of 1812? Mr. Peller better speed it up if you're going to finish the curriculum by June."

What were the odds? Who else but my father would care about what we were up to and what we had left to cover.

"Actually, we're up to Reconstruction," I stammered. "I was just reviewing."

Dad looked up and raised his eyebrows. "Reviewing?"

I just stood there silently.

Dad inhaled deeply. Then, with more effort than it would take him to run twice around the track, he raised himself from the chair.

"I guess midnight is not an ideal time for a chat," he mumbled, disappointed at my lie.

Then Murphy's Law, the one that says anything that can possibly go wrong will... struck again. The toe of his slipper caught on one of the photo album's ribbons sticking out from under my bed. He tripped but caught himself before he fell.

I rushed over to help him.

Embarrassed by his frailty, his face turned bright red.

"What is that on the floor?" he said angrily, kicking the album into the middle of the room. Before I could stop him, he bent down and picked up my baby book.

I could have used a swig of his anti-nausea medicine at that moment.

"Oh, that's my baby album," I said lightly, grateful for the dim light. "I was looking for a tray for Grandma in the den closet and I came across all this stuff..."

My voice was shaking but Dad didn't hear it. He wasn't listening to me. He was reading the page that was opened, studying the two appointment cards. He stared at the doctor's number I underlined just minutes before. Then he closed the book and handed it to me. His eyes were distant.

"Your time would be better spent looking back to 1870, not 2002," he said crisply. Then, without looking back or saying good night, he shuffled slowly out of the room, clutching his pills.

"Right," I answered, as I closed the door after him. If anyone asked how I felt at that moment, I don't think I'd be able to explain. Not only was I scared by how sick and weak he appeared; I was ashamed for upsetting him. There was also enormous relief at having survived such a close call. How could a person feel so many emotions at the same time without bursting?

"I can't help it, Dad," I sighed, as I copied down Dr. Prince's telephone number. "This has nothing to do with how hard I pray for you to get well. Or how much I love you. In fact, this has nothing to do with you at all."

CHAPTER SEVEN

I could hardly wait for the school day to end. This afternoon I'd finally have some answers. Tingly with hope, I raced up to my room and closed the door. My fingers shook as I picked up the telephone. Maybe Dr. Prince knew the name of the sperm bank my parents used. Maybe they'd have the donor's name on file. And maybe they'd tell me who he was. There was at least one too many maybes involved here for me to justify feeling optimistic, but how could I not even try.

As much as I had to make this call, I so wished I didn't want to. It would be better for everyone's sake if I forgot about donors and insemination. But I couldn't.

"Doctor's office, Mona speaking. How may I help you?" Mona sounded harried. I dug my nails into my palm.

"Oh, hi. I was wondering if I could speak to Dr. Prince. It's about a personal matter." My voice was shaking.

"I'm sorry, but Dr. Prince retired about five years ago. Is there someone else who can help you?"

My mind went blank.

"Can someone else help you?" Mona repeated, her clipped tone growing impatient.

"Dr. Prince delivered me twelve years ago," I began, "and I have a question he might be the only one who can answer." My throat felt so dry. "Is there any way you can tell me how I can get in touch with him?"

It was quiet on the other end. Then Mona, her voice a bit softer, said, "If you give me an idea of the kind of information you're looking for, perhaps Dr. Datz, the man to whom Dr. Prince sold his practice, can help you."

"Does he have the files from thirteen years ago?"

"What is it you want to know?"

"My mother was artificially inseminated. I'm looking for the name of the sperm bank she used. I thought maybe Dr. Prince might have recommended one to her."

"Please hold," instructed Mona. All of a sudden I was listening to *Seasons of Love* from *Rent*…the entire song. Finally, just as it was ending, she got back on the phone.

"Look dear, I just checked with Dr. Datz. All information between doctor and patient is privileged and could only be released to your mother, in person. He did say to tell you he doubts very much that Dr. Prince ever recommended one uh, facility over another. And he suggests you sit down and talk to your parents."

My heart sunk.

"I'm sorry but there's nothing we can do," Mona explained. "You forget that these are your mother's medical records, not yours. No doctor would ever give out this kind of private information."

Of course she was right.

"Well, thanks anyway, Mona," I said. "I appreciate your help."

"That's OK. Good luck to you…what's your name?"

"That's what I was hoping you'd help me find out," I said, as I hung up the phone.

———

"Did you hear, Sloane? Emma's going to be Dorothy in the third grade production of *The Wizard of Oz*." Mom's voice jolted me out of my reverie. I was sitting at the dinner table trying to figure a way around the dead end I encountered on the phone.

"You didn't eat much dinner tonight." Mom slinked up behind me and put her arms around my neck. "Want me to make you some eggs?" she offered. "Or a tuna melt sandwich?"

Since the last time we spoke weeks ago, she acted like she had no memory of our conversation. I tried to convince myself she couldn't help it. The same way I couldn't help feeling she could be doing a better job of being my mother. Just as the law finds an accomplice in a murder, whether he's just standing there or driving the getaway car, as guilty as the guy who pulled the trigger, she wasn't exactly blame-free for how desperately unsettled I felt. "No, I'm OK," I answered my tone light and frosty. "I'm just not very hungry."

It was amazing she didn't pick up on my leave-me-alone vibes. It wasn't always like that. Mom used to watch me walk off the school bus and know how my day had gone. Or tell by how I said hello on the phone what my mood was. No more.

"So did you hear what I said?" she repeated. "Emma's going to…"

"I heard, I heard," I said shortly.

Mom blinked a few times. "Well, we're all thrilled she got the part," she said before proceeding to clear the table.

It didn't feel good, hurting her feelings, but you'd think she, of all people, would understand how I felt. The kindest way to handle my ugly feelings about Emma was to ignore her. Everything from her *Hello Kitty* vitamins to her mammoth beanie boos collection, from her cheesy *One Direction* pencil case to her purple sneakers that flashed lights when she walked, disturbed me.

I passed the living room on the way upstairs to my room. Emma was on Dad's lap watching *The Simpsons*. Now that I knew the truth about how my family was made, the clues were so clear. He never once sat through *Seventh Heaven* with me when I was her age. The shows I liked were always too sappy for him.

"Sloane, Sloane," Emma called out. "Will you come to my show? It's going to be at night, in three weeks. I'm Dorothy. I get to sing two songs by myself."

I backed down a few steps and peeked my head in.

"What night is it?"

"I think Thursday." She held her face up like she expected to be kissed.

"We'll see." I said abruptly. "That's pretty close to my talent show so it depends how it's going." I turned back up the steps.

"If it's important to you," my father yelled after me. "I'm sure you could arrange it."

Right you are, Dad. Key words there were, "If it's important." Seeing my parents taking pictures, applauding and smiling proudly at their "real" child was way up there on the list of things I wouldn't want to miss. Right after walking barefoot in a snowstorm.

A few nights later Dad and I were alone in the house. Gram and Grandpa went with Mom to see Emma play the clarinet at the elementary school winter concert. Dad couldn't be in large crowds during flu season, so he had to stay home. And I begged off, saying I had a really hard math test the next day. Mom was actually relieved I was staying behind so Dad wouldn't be left alone.

After they'd gone, I went up to my room to fake study. Dad barely noticed. He was watching some bloody revenge movie on TV, where the bad guys get all the bullets, bombs and explosions they deserve.

I closed the door to my bedroom and decided to make this beauty night. It was time to stop envying Geena her gorgeous hair and glowing skin and do something about it. I washed my hair, then smeared on this dark, foul smelling hair conditioner that guaranteed, if you left it on for a half hour, a shine and texture to die for. I found a cucumber face mask in the bottom of my underwear drawer that Mom got as a sample months ago. While applying this green play-doh stuff all over my face and neck, I listened to the new Rihanna song. It smelled great and made my face feel all tingly. I was about to put on this cool, reddish-black nail polish that Selena Gomez wore on *Top Model* on TV when I heard my dad's voice.

I lowered the music and yelled down, "Did you call me?"

"Your mother just called. Emma forgot her sheet music. Would you find it on her desk and run it by the school? Mom will be waiting at the front door. It'll just take a few minutes."

The school was only a block and a half away. Ordinarily, it would be a moderate pain to go out in the cold and deliver the stupid music. But given my appearance, it was out of the question.

"Dad, I can't go. Emma'll have to look at the sheet music of the person sitting next to her. Or just pretend to play. She's always forgetting…"

The bedroom door swung open before I could finish the sentence.

Dad stood there in his Giants sweatshirt and saggy jeans. He looked at me and his mouth dropped.

"I'm a vision, I know," I said lightly, misreading what he was reacting to. "But you can see why I can't go." I wiggled my almost black thumb nail in front of him.

Dad's eyes narrowed and the muscle in his jaw began to twitch. I could feel myself deflating before his eyes.

"You said you were studying for a math test."

"I'm going to…" I stammered, "as soon as I wash this gunk off my face."

He stared at me.

"Would it have killed you to go your sister's concert? This was important to her."

I felt my cheeks get hot.

"Well, it wasn't important to me."

My father shook his head. "What's gotten into you?"

I just stared back at him.

"Answer me!" Dad demanded. "I don't understand where your attitude…or your tone… is coming from. Your mother keeps telling me this is how twelve-year-old girls are, that you're going through some kind of self-centered adolescent phase, but I don't buy it."

Thanks for the save, Mom. God, she must have been petrified when he started talking about me. I tried to remain calm. Every cell in my body screamed, "Tell him, tell him what he wants to know."

I curled my toes inside my sneakers.

"I've tried talking to you but you shut me down. You'd rather spend your time looking through baby albums, pretending to study." He was pumped now, using energy he couldn't afford to waste.

"You've been secretive and selfish, and I'm disappointed," he continued. "Your sister is in the third grade and she's shown more maturity than you have."

There it was, the "d" word…disappointed. His tirade reinforced everything I'd been thinking. Emma never disappointed him. A parent is naturally more forgiving of his own kid than someone else's. I bit the inside of my cheek, trying not to speak.

And then he said, "I wouldn't have imagined, especially at a time like this, that a daughter of mine…"

That was it. I did the best I could for as long as I could but like the restaurant sign that offers "all you can eat," that was all I could eat.

"Well, you have a better shot at getting the daughter you want with Emma," I interrupted.

"And what's that supposed to mean?" Dad asked, raising his eyebrows.

"I think you know what that means," I said wearily, swallowing over the lump growing in my throat. "Ignoring the facts doesn't change them… or make them go away."

Dad looked at me warily. "What are you saying?"

"I shouldn't have to explain anything to you. You should be explaining things to me," I went on, my voice rising. "Everything you just accused me of, I could say right back to you. You've been secretive and I'm disappointed in you too." I paused. Then I said quietly, "I guess this proves that not all behavior is inherited, huh?"

I saw the exact second he understood. Instead of leaning against the wall, as I'm sure he wanted to do, he drew himself up straighter. His jaw was twitching double-time. I watched his eyes slide past me, gazing off into space.

Then he turned his attention back to me.

"How dare you talk to me like this. I've given you no reason to disrespect me."

He made a move toward me but I didn't budge.

"I don't know what you're thinking…what you're planning to do with this information, but I forbid you to…"

"To what, find out who I am?" I felt my heart beating in my throat but my voice was surprisingly strong. "That's all I want to do Dad, please try to understand. The last thing in the world I want to do is upset you but…"

"You…are…Sloane…Davis," Dad hissed through clenched teeth. "That's all you need to know." He was breathing hard.

I looked at him. "You always tell me to go with my gut…to listen to what it tells me. My gut tells me what you want me to do, to forget this whole thing, is not what's best for me."

I don't know where I found the strength to confront him.

"How did you find out?" he whispered.

"It's not important," I said bleakly. "I got suspicious when they tested Emma's blood before mine to see if it was a match with yours."

He nodded. "I thought of that," he said more to himself than to me.

I stared at him and breathed, "Can you explain why you never told me?"

There was a long silence.

Finally Dad stuck out his chin. "Because what good could come of making you feel insecure?" He looked me straight in the eye. " I rocked you to sleep, and when that didn't work, I danced you across the living room floor for hours till you closed your eyes. You were our child and there was no reason on earth to confuse the issue."

"Why did..."

"Look, Sloane, I am not on trial here and I'm not going to answer any more questions. Your mother and I handled this situation the best way we knew how." His hands, curled into two white knuckled fists, hung at his sides. "It's obvious you're too upset right now to see things clearly." He cleared his throat as if he were giving a speech to his students. "It's unfortunate you had to find out this way. But it would be a mistake to pursue this further."

Without another word he turned and left the room. How I wished he said he was sorry he never told me. Or admit that he didn't tell me because he was uncomfortable with the whole idea. Or say that he understood why I felt so strongly about looking for the sperm donor, even if he didn't want me to.

For what felt like a long time I stood there numbly, with a tar-like substance on my head, grease on my face and still sticky almost black nail polish, drying on one thumb. I couldn't discount a stray alien claiming fatherhood at that moment.

CHAPTER EIGHT

It was dumb of me to bring it up.

"So I'm thinking of getting one of those Abercrombie zippered jackets… maybe in light green, what do you think?" Molly and I were sitting at my computer in my bedroom trying to find out how my dad who couldn't father a child, was suddenly able to. We googled artificial insemination.

"Truthfully? Just the idea," Molly said, wrinkling her nose as she expertly clicked through a dozen research sites, "of you all minty and matchy with Geena's peachy pink and Rebecca's baby blue makes me want to puke."

"Please don't be that way," I begged.

"Same to you," Molly retorted. "Please don't be that way."

In a few minutes the information we discovered released the tension between us. We learned the process of artificial insemination was first used to breed cattle. Only in the last fifty years was frozen sperm used to create human beings. More than seven hundred sperm banks practice donor insemination. I wondered how many children they made through the years knew how they came to be. And if they did find out, how they felt about it.

"Well, it says here almost fifty percent of the problems married couples have conceiving a baby come from the husbands."

That was a surprise.

"Smoking and drinking and extra weight are factors in creating some men's problems," she continued.

"No, my father has always been an athlete. Since he was a teenager, he's always been in great shape."

"Oh... here it is then," Molly squealed as she read aloud. "High intensity exercise can raise body temperature... and warm body temperature is related to low sperm count."

That made sense. I knew in college my father was an All American lacrosse player and after that, a ranked racquetball player. My mother used to say he spent more time in the gym than out of it.

"So maybe later when my father began teaching and had less time to devote to exercise, his sperm count went up."

"Sure, that's a possibility," Molly agreed. "So does knowing why they used a sperm bank make it any easier?"

"Not really," I sighed.

Molly clicked away for a few minutes.

"Look, Sloane, this article quotes the head urologist at New York Hospital. He said 'It's my experience that only the most solid marriages, those couples with a good basis for communicating, are interested in artificial insemination.'"

My eyes got blurry.

'In all my years of practice,' Molly continued, 'I've never had one couple come back to me and say that they made the wrong decision.'

"Well, they're not going to march into his office years later and tell him woops, we made a mistake."

"Come on, Sloane." Molly pushed her chair away from the keyboard and turned to face me. She folded her arms across her chest. "Tell me that you think your parents are sorry you were born."

"No, not really. But you can't tell me my father wasn't ten times more excited when my mother became pregnant with Emma."

"You're never going to know how he felt if you don't talk to him," Molly said gently.

"My father's not exactly approachable about this topic," I said thickly, grabbing a tissue from my night table.

For the hundredth time my mind flashed on the difference in my father's reaction to my making honor roll compared to when Emma scored the winning goal in soccer.

"So you're saying you agree it's right never to tell a kid the truth?

That what she doesn't know won't hurt her?"

Molly sighed. "I could tell you my opinion and my father's opinion and 500 other doctor's opinions but that's not what's going to make you feel better. What you want won't be found in how many other people agree with you."

I blew my nose.

"Could you just look up the names of the sperm banks in New York my parents might have used in 2002? There couldn't have been too many then."

"I'll try but I'm telling you you're heading in the wrong direction…"

I stood up quickly. "Please don't think I'm not grateful for all your help," I said more curtly than I meant to, "but deciding whether to track down my real father doesn't feel like a choice… it's something I have to do."

"We all have choices," Molly said as she picked her jacket off the floor. "We can be grateful for what we have… or we can feel miserable about what we don't."

My spine stiffened.

"What's that supposed to mean?" I couldn't help noticing how wrong Molly's old green Jantzen backpack looked compared to the little pink Kate Spade bags Geena and Rebecca carried. My mind flashed to what happened yesterday.

"Let's go guys, we have a lot of work to do today," I said clapping my hands as I climbed on stage in the auditorium.

I was up late putting the finishing touches on the next thirty second combination. Rebecca was finishing up a phone conversation and Molly was lacing up her sneakers. Geena hopped up and stood facing me with her back to the audience.

"I've been thinking," she began, whispering so the others wouldn't hear. "I know you agree the two of us are the better dancers. What if we stand in front, not blocking anyone or anything but just a few feet ahead of them… what do you think?"

What did I think? I thought the four of us should be spaced across the stage in one line. I choreographed all the moves for that configuration. It didn't make a difference that we were the stronger dancers if we did the routine right.

"I know you have trouble with this sort of thing...telling people stuff they don't want to hear... that's cause you're a mush." She grinned and came closer. "Luckily that's no biggie for me. I'll tell them if you want. I don't mind being the bad guy."

Just then Mr. Altman turned on the music and I never had a chance to answer. The memory made me uncomfortable.

"It's like all of a sudden who you are isn't good enough." Molly's voice brought me back.

"I don't know what you're talking about," I protested.

Just then message from Geena popped on the screen.

Wanna go shopping Saturday? No offense but those shoes have to go!

She was talking about the fake Uggs I bought a few months before ...the shoes that were on Molly's feet that very instant.

"I could understand if you were this upset about your dad being sick or your mom being so stressed or your sister being scared... but you're not," Molly said in a rush, pretending to ignore the words on the screen. "You act like everyone who loves you purposely did something horrible to hurt you. All you talk about is stupid sperm." Molly gulped, her cheeks red. "And as much as I want to feel bad for you, I can't."

"I never asked you to feel bad for me."

"Well, that works out great then, doesn't it," Molly snapped as she grabbed her things and opened the bedroom door.

The front door slammed shut. I sat motionless on my bed. Then I got up to empty my laundry basket. Usually that basket could sit in my room for days till I wear all the clean clothes in it but today emptying it beat thinking about Molly being mad at me and it being all my fault.

I put down my nightgown and called her. It rang and rang till her message came on. That was unusual.

"You know what to do...I'll call you right back" she promised.

I did. Then I waited all night but she didn't.

CHAPTER NINE

Dad came down with the flu about a week after our blow up. He had to go back into the hospital for a transfusion. No one said it out loud, but I was sure they all blamed me because he went out into the winter night air to deliver Emma's sheet music. Mom tried to make me feel better, explaining it was an old wives' tale that you could get the flu from being out in the cold. But I didn't believe her.

I was rummaging in the basement, looking for who knows what, some hint about where to go next, when I heard her voice.

"Sloane, are you down there?" yelled Emma. Dad was nodding off on his recliner and Mom left for the airport to take Grandma and Grandpa back to Florida. The cold weather was really rough on them and Dad insisted they return home.

"Is it OK if I come down there? I want to show you something." Without waiting for an answer, she came flying down the steps. "What are you doing in the basement?" she asked, peering over my shoulder.

"What are you doing in the basement?" I echoed.

She held up her spelling paper with *100%, Great Job!* written across the top.

"Look what I got on my spelling test," she said proudly.

"When was the last time you didn't get a 100 on a spelling test?" I said suspiciously. "What's so special about this test?"

"Why aren't you coming to my play?" she went on, ignoring my question. "I want you to see me. I wear the sickest costume. And I sing all by myself."

"I wish I could," I lied, returning my attention to the half emptied carton of old toys on the floor. Had to give the kid credit. She was relentless when she wanted something.

"You could if you wanted. I heard Mommy say that to Daddy."

"Is that right?" I said evenly, keeping my eyes on the pile in front of me. "Well, maybe Mommy's wrong."

"She said she didn't know what to do with you. Dad said to leave you alone, that you'll snap out of it yourself, but Mom said she's afraid that won't happen for a long time."

I turned to look at Emma. She was standing a few inches away from me wearing purple Sleeping Beauty pajamas with feet and a glittery hot pink scrunchi in her hair.

"Why are you telling me this?"

"Because I don't know what to do with you either. What do you have to snap out of?"

She waited, hands on her hips, for my response.

I looked away. If it weren't so sad, it'd be really funny.

"At first I thought you were just being mean to me," Emma continued. "But you're mad at everybody... all the time."

She stopped. Then she cupped her hand around her mouth, put her face to my ear, and whispered, "Are you doing really bad in school?"

If I had a sister four years older than I was, and she treated me the way I was treating Emma, I'd never want to be anywhere near her. She was something else, this kid.

"Nothing's wrong. I just need my space. Maybe sometime when you're a little older we can talk about what that feels like."

"So if nothing's wrong, please come to my play. I have the biggest part."

I shook my head.

"Please... I'll come to your dance if you come to my show," she pleaded.

"I can't," I repeated, this time in a tone that let her know further discussion was useless.

"I know you can, Sloane. You just don't want to," she sniffled, finally breaking down and sounding like an eight year old. "Molly is coming and Zachary is just an elf in the chorus. I wish she was my sister." She punched me hard on my back and darted for the stairs. "Everybody's whole family is coming, except mine. I hate you," she yelled, slamming the door at the top of the steps.

Can't blame her, I thought as I started putting the old cardboard boxes back on the dusty shelves. Can't blame her one bit.

———

I liked getting to the auditorium for dance rehearsal at least fifteen minutes before the others. It gave me a chance to get the music ready and plan out exactly what we'd be working on. Today I was surprised to see Geena's books and jacket on a seat in the front row when I arrived.

"Hey," Geena announced, returning from the bathroom, carrying a little makeup bag like the ones my mom uses when she goes out. Freshly blushed and glossed, she approached with a big grin. She wearing a tight tee shirt that said *I'm 99% sure I'm a Disney princess*; I wore an oversized sweatshirt that said *Tootsie Roll...* and she made herself pretty for me?

"So I thought if I got here early and it was just the two of us, I could show you those moves I told you about."

"Sure," I said dropping my eyes down to admire the brand new pair of black hip hop sneakers she was wearing. "Let's see what you've got."

Geena put on a song I loved from *Teen Beach Movie*. Then I watched as she strode up on stage and did a really cool thirty second routine.

"Do it again," I asked.

I watched carefully, dissecting the impressive intricate combination.

"Come up here with me. It looks even better when two people do it," Geena said, flashing another Julia Roberts smile.

I climbed up next to her and followed her lead. Then I added a shimmy and a roll. She copied perfectly. Then she added a turn and I repeated it. We went over and over the combination for the rest of the three-minute song till we were both sweating. Without saying a word I walked over and replayed the song. After three more times, we worked out a new ending for our routine. Geena laughed out loud and put her hand up in the air for a fist bump.

"That was so much fun," she said, breathing hard. "You're an amazing dancer."

"You too," I said. "That was really incredible. Did it take you long to come up with it?

"Actually yes. Forever. I knew if I wanted to impress you, it had to be better than just good."

I tried not to smile as I rummaged through my backpack looking for something to mop up my sweaty face. Geena handed me a tissue she pulled out of her tiny Coach bag. It smelled like tangerines.

Just then Molly appeared. Since our words a few days before, it was just easier to pretend nothing had changed. A friendship in trouble we could handle. No friendship at all was not an option. She pulled out jazz shoes from her bag and sat on the floor to put them on.

"You should definitely come over sometime so we can choreograph together," Geena said a bit louder than she had to.

Before I could answer, Molly walked over.

"Hope I'm not interrupting anything," she said, turning her back to Geena. "I was thinking maybe we could stop at the elementary school on the way home today and watch the kids rehearse. Don't you think they would love that?"

I wondered if Emma told Zachary I wasn't coming to the show and this was Molly's way of making me change my mind. If it was, it wasn't working. Why couldn't she just butt out?

When she saw me hesitate, she went on. "If not this afternoon, maybe another day." Then she turned to Geena. "Sloane's little sister is Dorothy in The Wizard of Oz... she's the most adorable..."

"...pain in my butt" I finished her sentence.

Molly blinked. Then she shook her head

"Sorry for mistaking you for someone who cares about more than herself," she said under her breath.

"That's not fair," I answered. "It's not like we haven't had this discussion before."

"We haven't," she said flatly. "And don't worry, we never will again." Then she turned and walked down the steps to the back of the auditorium..

"Jeez, what's with her? I thought she was your best friend," Geena whispered.

I shrugged.

"I know you two have hung out for a really long time but she's kind of possessive, don't you think? That was so obviously an excuse, interrupting us that way."

I realized I was clenching my teeth. How dare Molly make my hard life harder? That's not what friends do.

"By the way, I'm not a fan of little kids either," Geena continued, rolling her eyes. "I'm lucky I have a big sister who ignores me enough not to notice I borrow her clothes and try on her make up all the time."

I smiled weakly. So perhaps there were two queen bees living at Geena's house. I forced myself to put on the music and focus on the new combination. Luckily everyone caught on quickly. Molly was three feet away from me but I missed her.

CHAPTER TEN

"Wish me luck," ordered Emma, over breakfast the morning of the play. It wasn't even 7:15 and she was already dressed. She was so hyped up, she didn't realize she was eating a healthy cereal, rather than the sweet one she was entitled to that day. Mom had a rule ever since I was little. One day you were allowed to eat the cereal of your choice; the next, you had to choose a cereal without sugar. Emma ate Special K yesterday. This morning, the latest marshmallow, frosted, movie-tie-in, taste-sensation was hers for the asking.

"Good luck," I repeated, with a small smile. "You can come up to my room and tell me all about it when you get home."

I wished she didn't look so cute and vulnerable, suddenly making missing her performance a tough test of my resolve. Besides, I reasoned, there'll be so many people around telling her how terrific she was, she wouldn't even notice I wasn't there.

"Are you sure..." she began, then stopped herself, realizing she had a better shot finding one last raisin in her empty cereal bowl than getting me to change my mind. My mother looked at me but didn't say a word. I never imagined getting my own way would leave me feeling so empty.

Anyway, I made plans for tonight. Having the house to myself, I got up the nerve to invite Geena over after rehearsal to share my Chanukah present, the two disc set of Beyonce's seventeen videos from her latest album. We were sure there'd be at least a few moves worth stealing.

Mom left for work and Dad, most unusually, hadn't come downstairs yet. The thought crossed my mind he was so angry with me for not going, that he purposely waited until I left before coming down for breakfast. If that's how he felt, it actually wasn't a bad idea.

The day passed in a flash. I made sure Geena and I stayed after school till 5:00, so the house would be empty when we got home. Mom and Dad were taking Emma out for an early dinner before the show, the first time in months Dad would eat in a restaurant. I explained to Geena this was the night of Emma's performance, the one Molly and I had the fight about. She didn't seem to care. Then I microwaved some popcorn for while we watched the video and took out some frozen mac and cheese for our dinner.

―――――――――

The phone rang a few times but I ignored it. They'd leave a message.

"I hate to pick up my parents' phone, don't you?" I said. "It's never anyone you want to speak to."

After we watched the video we decided to incorporate two of Beyonce's steps into our routine.

When we were done, Geena bent down and pulled two scarves out of her book bag. She tied one across my forehead.

"See where you wear it?" she instructed. "Down low, so your hair doesn't show, right above your eyebrows." Then she pulled my sweat pants down to just below my belly button. "Go look at yourself."

I ran to the mirror in the front hall. Who was that cool looking girl, the one with her pants folded over, her flat belly showing just a bit, and the neat scarf carelessly, perfectly framing her face? The one with the most popular girl in seventh grade smiling proudly behind her?

"This is good, right Sloane?"

I wasn't sure whether by 'this' she meant my new look or the choreography or us. It really didn't matter. This was all good.

I moved the coffee table out of the way and we got busy fine tuning our new steps. After an hour, we were exhausted. We ate dinner and Geena called her mom to pick her up.

"Did you see *Moulin Rouge*? *Save the Last Dance*? *Mad Hot*

Ballroom?" she asked as she put on her coat.

I shook my head.

"I always wanted to watch them with someone who loves to dance as much as I do," she smiled, leaning over to give me a hug. "We should do that sometime."

"Sure, sounds great," I agreed, just as the doorbell rang. And rang and rang, like someone was keeping his finger on the bell. Geena shrugged her shoulders.

"That's not my mom," she said, "she'd never get out of the car."

"Who's there?" I called out.

"It's me," answered Emma. Her voice sounded ragged, like she'd been crying.

When I opened the door, she rushed in right past me, almost knocking me down. She ran straight up to her room and slammed the door. I heard her sobbing. Standing silently at the front door was Molly.

"Can I come in for a minute?" she said through gritted teeth.

"Of course," I said, stepping aside to let her in. I didn't release my grip on the door knob.

She stared first at Geena, then at me, the naked rage behind her eyes cutting through the air like a knife.

"What happened? Where are my parents? Why is Emma so upset?" My voice was shaking.

"Your parents dropped Emma off at school after they ate. They couldn't stay because your father was feeling faint and your mother wanted to get him to the hospital to check him out."

"Oh," I said. My mind was racing. "So they didn't see her?"

"No, Sloane, they left before the play started."

A car honked. Geena picked up her things and walked to the front door where Molly was standing. It was the first time I ever saw her uncomfortable. She flashed a sympathetic smile and ran out without saying a word.

"We could've gone together," Molly continued after the door slammed. "I didn't mention it to you today because you've been in such a foul mood. Then when you didn't show up, I called the house but no one answered." She took a deep breath. "Anyway in case you care,

Emma was great tonight but she's devastated no one in her family was there to see her."

I felt dizzy and leaned weakly against the door.

"You obviously had something more important to do," Molly said coldly.

I stood there praying for some words to answer her, to explain, to excuse what I did, but none arrived. I felt sick.

"Emma made me keep calling you, supposedly to tell you about your dad," she went on, ignoring my silence. "But I'm sure it was really to get you to come see her."

I nodded dumbly. The source of my anger toward Emma and Molly and whoever else I blamed for my misery, dried up.

"Look, Sloane, I know you hate when I get bossy and preachy..."

"Go on," I mumbled. Whatever she would say, I had it coming.

"When I first walked into the auditorium and read the program, I looked around for you and your parents. It never occurred to me that you wouldn't be there."

"Look, Molly, I don't think you could ever understand..."

"It's not me you have to explain to," Molly interrupted.

"If you lived in this house and saw how she drinks up all the attention...," I began, then stopped. Even I didn't believe whatever it was I was going to say. It made no difference. Molly didn't hear me anyway.

"No matter how pissed you are at your parents, Emma was standing in a corner all by herself at intermission. She was the star of the whole production and she was the only kid backstage all alone." The memory of that moment got her angry all over again and she started talking louder and faster.

"You have to deal with this whole insemination thing in a better way, Sloane. Not by picking on an eight year old."

"Are you finished?" I said, shoving my hands in my pockets.

"Almost." Molly swallowed hard. "You are my best friend in life but I have to tell you, you did a terrible thing. Emma's a terrific kid and she didn't deserve what happened tonight."

"You know I would have been there if I knew my parents couldn't make it," I said lamely. "I really thought she'd be so distracted she wouldn't miss me." I forced myself to look into Molly's eyes.

She shook her head. "Maybe you've tried to convince yourself that's true but Emma told me she asked you ten times to please be there." She met my gaze and held it. "Please at least be honest with yourself first before you say anything to her," she said quietly.

" I will." I croaked, my voice thick with emotion, "Thanks… and thanks for bringing her home,"

I closed the door and without thinking, found myself in the kitchen making hot chocolate. It wasn't possible to feel more like a slime ball than I did at that moment. I stirred in an extra teaspoon of sugar and brought it upstairs. There was no sound coming from Emma's room.

I knocked on the door. "Emma, can I come in?"

No response. I tried the door but it was locked.

"I heard you were amazing tonight. Molly couldn't stop raving. She said she never knew you had such a great voice." I put my ear to the door and could hear her crying softly.

"Please, Emma, let me in. I made you some hot chocolate."

"You should've come, Sloane. We called and you wouldn't even pick up the phone. I don't want to talk to you, ever."

I stood outside her door, holding the hot cup for a long time. I felt a heaviness I never experienced before. It took a minute to give it a name…*shame*. I had been embarrassed a million times in my life: I'd made mistakes and told hundreds of little lies. God knows I've felt ugly and clumsy a million times more than I've felt smart and pretty. But I never felt this…inexcusably, thoroughly ashamed of myself. What a safe target I chose. Not someone who could fight back, but my baby sister.

"I don't blame you, Emma, I said softly. "I wouldn't want to talk to me either. I'll leave your hot chocolate on the banister."

I walked into my room, picked up the phone and forced myself to listen to the messages.

Before the ones from Molly and Emma there was one from my mother.

"Hi, Sloane. It's a few minutes before 7:00 and we're at the hospital. They just examined Daddy and decided to keep him here for a few days. His white blood cell count was very high." Her voice cracked. "I'll be home as soon as he's settled in a room. Please, please if you hear this in the next half hour, rush over to the elementary school to watch Emma. She was heartbroken when we had to leave. See you later."

I lay on my bed for a long time without putting on the light. Till I heard my mother come home.

I opened my door as she got to the top of the steps. She looked exhausted.

"Were you able to make the show?" The first words out of her mouth.

"No."

She sighed. "The doctor said Dad will be home in a few days. This is just routine for leukemia patients." She walked straight into her room without another word.

As I heard her close her bedroom door, the thought occurred to me that we had to be the three most miserable females under one roof on the entire planet. We awoke the next morning to find the blood tests they took in the hospital revealed my dad was no longer in remission. The leukemia had returned. Plans were made to schedule a bone marrow transplant as soon as possible. I watched as Emma prepared to put her marrow where her mouth was, and get ready to save his life.

CHAPTER ELEVEN

Mom got busy right away, transforming Dad's hospital room into a place he'd be comfortable spending the next two months. Since he was entering what they called "modified protective isolation," and was forbidden to leave his room, she wanted to make sure his living space at The Transplant Hilton would be as cheery and familiar as possible.

First thing, she angled the bed so he could see out the window. She bought his pillow and their comforter, a signed photo of this year's football team and five or six framed pictures of all of us. She tried to bring in some plants but they weren't allowed. There was a stack of this month's car magazines on the night table next to his bed along with every sports publication on the newsstand.

But a thousand comfy touches couldn't hide the tubes and wires coming out of Dad's chest. Once they started the heavy-duty chemo… ten to twenty times what he already withstood…all of his medication and nourishment would come through those lines. One exited from the right side, just below his waist. Two others exited from his chest and just hung there.

Every wire was connected to an I.V. pole we immediately named Ivan. Ivan had a body made of square metal monitors, one for this chest and one for his stomach, with numbers that went up as his medicine went down. He'd sing a computerized rendition of Beethoven's Fifth whenever Dad's I.V. bags were on empty. Ivan would be Dad's faithful companion, following him everywhere, until he was ready to leave the hospital.

"Gimme your biggest guns," he told the doctors grimly. "Don't hold back. Let's kill every last one of those freaking cells."

"That's the idea, Neil. You know this isn't going to be easy…"

"If it were easy, it wouldn't work, I know that," Dad answered shortly. "When can we get started?"

"Tomorrow. In the morning we'll extract Emma's marrow. We'll start you on seven days of chemo, followed by one day's rest. Then we'll transplant Emma's marrow in you."

"If only there were some other way…" Dad's voice trailed off. "This is a hell of a thing for an eight year old to have to go through."

"Emma's going to be fine. I promise you," Dr. Ruden smiled reassuringly. "Everybody's making a big fuss over her upstairs and she's all set to come to your rescue."

Although she'd only be in the hospital overnight, Emma's room was filled with flowers. Grandma and Grandpa sent some. So did Molly's family and Emma's teacher. On her bed was a shopping bag with Julie, her favorite American Girl doll, along with her ancient baby blanket, a bag of pink lemonade jelly beans and this month's New Moon magazine.

The evening before the procedure, Mom and I sat on her bed, waiting for the doctor to come in with last minute instructions. Mom was going to spend the night on a cot in Emma's room.

"Are you sure you're OK sleeping alone in the house tonight" she said that afternoon. "I hate the idea. I don't understand why you're not staying over at Molly's. Are you sure…."

"I'm fine Mom," I said, cutting her off mid sentence, mortified at how my measure of discomfort, being by myself overnight, paled next to Emma's sacrifice. We had this conversation at least ten times this week until finally Mom gave up. She had no idea I hadn't spoken to Molly since the night of Emma's play. I didn't like adding to her worries but there was no other place I'd rather be than in my own bed. Anyway, it seemed kind of fitting, the three of them together at the hospital, and me, home alone.

"So, Emma, I bought you a present," I said, tossing a bag into her lap. She left it there, unopened.

"Mom, tell me again what'll happen if I need some bone marrow and I gave all mine to Daddy?" she asked, biting her lip.

"They only need a tiny bit of your marrow, sweetheart," Mom answered patiently. "And that will replenish itself in just a few weeks."

"I'm going to be fast asleep, right?" This conversation, word for word, had taken place at least five times in the last two days.

"Right."

"And when I wake up, you'll be in the room, right?"

"Right."

She looked so small lying there.

"Aren't you going to open Sloane's present?" Mom asked, attempting to change the subject.

But Emma wasn't finished asking questions. Or punishing me.

"When I wake up, can I go home?"

"Maybe. We'll see how you feel."

"And my back will be sore but I can still walk?"

"Of course you can walk. You'll be tired from the general anesthesia and sore where they removed your marrow, but you'll be as good as new in just a few days." Mom's voice sounded bright and comforting but I could see she was worried. We both knew it would take twenty to thirty punctures to extract enough marrow.

"Since when do you have the self control not to rip open a present?" I asked. "Usually you attack wrapping paper with your teeth."

Emma looked up at me. "I'll open it. I'm just a little nervous now, that's all."

I had to look away. She was being so good about this whole thing. No tears. No play acting. If I didn't know better, I'd swear she was intentionally being perfect just so I should feel worse. I shook my head, embarrassed that thought even crossed my mind. And I had the nerve to call *her* self-centered.

Emma ignored the card and ripped open the box. It was my IPOD uploaded with her favorite, Katy Perry's, latest soundtrack. Her eyes opened wide.

"Thanks, Sloane."

"Read the card," I said, clearing my throat. It was a blank card with a picture of Dorothy's ruby red slippers on the cover. Inside I'd written, *I can't tell you how bad I feel about missing your big night. Maybe sometime soon we can talk about it. I know you must have heard from a lot of people how great you were. But you've never been more of a star than you are right now.*" I signed it, "*Your extremely sorry sister and very proud admirer, Sloane.*"

As if she knew how important it was to me that she read what it said, she yawned and said, "Later. I'll save it for later."

"You better go home, honey," Mom said looking at her watch. "I don't want you walking into an empty house late at night."

"OK," I said reluctantly. "I'll go." I bent over to give Emma a kiss. She lifted her cheek but kept her hands at her sides. It could take more than some music and a weak apology to earn a hug.

"I'll be sending positive thoughts at 8:00 tomorrow morning. Concentrate and you'll feel them," I said straightening up.

"But I'll be sleeping."

"Just concentrate, you'll feel them."

As I left the room, I heard her asking my mother whether it's possible to concentrate while you're sleeping.

When I got home I went straight up to my room. With my door shut, I could pretend this was like any other Tuesday night. Except now the silence demanded I go over what happened that afternoon. My mind replayed a conversation I overheard in Dad's hospital room. I was coming back from the bathroom and stopped at his door when I heard Mom and Dad talking.

"Karen, I know how you hate discussing these things, but I can't go through with this unless I'm sure you know where all our papers are." He sounded nonchalant, as if he were talking about what to watch on TV.

"I know, Neil."

"All the life insurance policies and financial information is in the vault. Along with the stock certificates for Sloane's college."

"I know, Neil."

"And my will…"

"Please, I know where everything is. I put it there, remember?" Mom's voice sounded raspy, like that day on the phone with the doctor.

"OK, OK. I just needed to be sure. It's irresponsible not to at least admit there's a chance I might not make it."

"You're going to make it. You and Emma are a wonderful match. God wouldn't have seen to that unless He intended you to get well. You're young and strong and motivated…and you're going to be fine." Her voice cracked.

It got quiet after that and I couldn't hear what they were saying. I pictured them holding on to each other, like the books say, "for dear life." I continued walking down the hall, wishing with all my heart that I had someone to hold on to.

"For dear life." It wasn't the first time I realized how seriously ill Dad was. But knowing something, and letting yourself feel it, are two different things. I started thinking about the most random things… how he orders a ton of extra pickles on his hamburgers, how we always groan, then laugh, at the same three stupid knock- knock jokes he's told over and over, how he always stands in the same place and takes the exact same picture of us every year blowing out our birthday candles.

That night I let go of the fierce tears that had been pushing at me from inside. I prayed that night in the house all by myself. I prayed for Dad to recover, for Emma not to hurt too much, for Mom to have some peace of mind. And for me to understand what had become of my life. The outside lights were turned on. The thermostat was turned way down. All the doors were double-locked. Sleep well, Dad, all the chores are done.

Chapter Twelve

Emma came home two days later. Although tired and achy, she was in remarkably good spirits. The editor of the high school newspaper where dad worked came by.

"So how did you feel when you realized it was up to you to donate the bone marrow that could save your father's life?" asked the somber English major as she placed a tape recorder on the table between them. "Were you scared?"

"A little," Emma said slowly. Playing Dorothy was a stepping stone for such an occasion. Propped up with three pillows on the living room couch, she was covered with the multi-colored afghan Grandma made years ago. We all used it whenever we felt crummy. "But the doctor said I'd be sleeping so it wouldn't hurt."

"What was your dad's reaction when he found out you volunteered to do this? That must have been a pretty emotional moment."

"Not really. We didn't talk about it much."

The reporter raised her eyebrows.

"My daddy's very sick," Emma said sharply. "If I were very sick, he'd give me his marrow." She glanced over to Mom who shook her head approvingly. "When he gets better, we'll probably talk about it."

She really was smart for an eight year old.

I left the room as Emma launched into a detailed description of every moment of the two-day stay she remembered…and a few she imagined.

Her ordeal was over and dad's was just beginning. As soon as

Emma's marrow was harvested, he began his week of high dose chemotherapy. Now when I visited him, I had to put on a hospital gown and wash my hands in a small sink outside his room. Then when I got inside, I had to wash again to make sure I wasn't bringing in any stray bacteria. As Ivan administered the drops of deadly elixir into his veins, his condition immediately worsened. Stripped of all immunity against infection, the most innocent germ could lead to a life and death struggle.

Thankfully, mixed in with the cancer killing drugs was a variety of tranquilizers. The combination left him comfortably woozy. He knew where he was and who I was... but his memory for detail was gone. Relaxation agreed with him.

"Sloane," he whispered one afternoon, five days into the treatment, "is she gone?"

"Who?"

"Florence Frightingale, the nurse with one eyebrow across her forehead."

I started to laugh. "Yes, Dad, she's gone. I think she's only here in the morning and now it's six o'clock at night."

"Good."

"Why don't you like her? Isn't she nice to you?"

"She's OK, I guess, but she tells the most awful stories. The last one was about a guy who bent down one day, stepped on the end of his catheter without realizing it, then stood up and yanked the whole thing out of his chest."

"Oh my God, how terrible! Why would she tell you story like that?"

Dad shrugged.

"What did you say to her?"

"I thanked her for sharing."

We both laughed. Dad seemed to have no memory of what transpired between us in the last few weeks. What a gift it was for both of us, his failure to remember. Like turning back time.

"By the way," Dad began, "knowing you're taking care of things at home helps me concentrate on killing these bastard cells."

I tried not to smile. Dad in his right mind would never curse in front of me.

"You and me, we're the detail people in the family." He looked at me through glassy eyes. "Your mother and Emma have a lot of strong qualities but they're easily distracted, you know what I mean. "He yawned. "They forget about the bottom line."

"Close your eyes, Dad. Rest for a few minutes."

"That's why people trust us," he muttered, drifting off to sleep. "cause we're responsible."

I sat for a long while, staring at his face. There wasn't a trace of the macho, control freak whose chest hair always leaped over the neck of his tee shirt. It was all so confusing. More painful than watching him suffer... or being furious with him... was hearing him say how much alike we were. If he was right, and people could trust us, why were we having such a hard time trusting each other?

After a week of near lethal doses of chemo, Dad was injected with Emma's healthy bone marrow. The doctor said it would take two to four weeks to manufacture enough white blood cells, red blood cells and platelets to return him to feeling like a human being. The first few days he was just very weak. Then the honeymoon was over.

The nausea and diarrhea were horrific but the fevers were worse. Fevers meant the presence of infection, and without any white blood cells to do combat, even the most innocent of activities...opening the mail, brushing his teeth, blowing his nose...could kill him.

"What's taking my blood count so long to come back?" he asked the nurse morosely. "I've been here almost five weeks and the numbers aren't budging."

If he behaved the same way he did on his first hospital stay, he'd be yelling at her, like it was her fault. But this time there was more fear than fight in his tone.

"They'll come back, Mr. Davis, just have patience."

"But what if they don't come back? What if I can never leave this room?" His voice was quivering.

Seeing him so scared was shocking.

"They're young, Emma's white blood cells, they're probably just finding their way," I said lamely. "Give them a chance...."

The nurse smiled, nodding in agreement.

74

"I know you're both trying to make me feel better," Dad said, still looking out the window. "But I'd rather be alone now, if you don't mind."

For the first time since Dad got sick, terror grabbed at my throat. I cried all the way home.

Each day I tried to pretend what went on in that hospital room had little bearing on the rest on my life. I was afraid Dad's dark mood was like quicksand, and if I allowed myself to get too close, I'd sink down with him. Safe as long as I kept moving, my grades were as good as ever and I didn't miss a single rehearsal. If I didn't talk much, nobody seemed to notice. I was fine living my fake life until dark when I ran out of places to go... and it was time to be alone with my thoughts.

At night in my room, I missed Molly painful amounts. I flipped through the channels but nothing on TV held my interest. There was nothing scarier on any channel than the nightmare that was my life. After a half hour of cleaning out my underwear drawer, I was desperate for distraction. I decided to fill the silence by calling... and confiding in... Geena. What was the worst that could happen, I thought, dialing her number. She wouldn't be sympathetic? It was worth the gamble, anything to keep the demons at bay.

I was relieved when she sounded genuinely happy to hear my voice.

"You sound terrible," she said, picking up on my tone immediately, "What's wrong?"

My head started to throb. Here it was, the overdue opportunity to tell my wretched, crazy, sad story... to someone whose concern already felt like a hug.

I took a deep breath.

"Please, Sloane, tell me," she implored.

The whole tale poured out... the artificial insemination, Emma, my dad's transplant, my grandparents' reaction, the quest for my biological father, all of it.

"Wow," Geena breathed, when I finally stopped talking. "That's a lot."

"Yeah, it is," I agreed.

Then very quietly Geena said, "In a weird way, you're lucky. I mean

I'd trade in my dad for either one of yours. My father is a jerk who left when I was four. Even then I didn't miss him." She paused. "Once in a while he comes by to take me and my sister out for dinner... but he always brings along a woman half his age to make sure we can never talk about anything that means anything."

I listened, not really surprised and not really minding that somehow the conversation became all about Geena.

"That's not all. My stepdad is nice in a nerdy kind of way but he has these two obnoxious teenage sons who come over every other weekend and my mother makes me be nice to them. One tried to kiss me last summer. It was gross."

"Ugh."

"You know I don't think either of my dads particularly cares that much about me," Geena confided. "It's not like they ever did stuff like read me a bedtime story or teach me how to ride a two wheeler." She hesitated. "In a way it makes it easier. One is horrid and one is boring but neither has the power to make me cry anymore."

Wow. So what was the lesson here? That life is much more complicated... and painful... but better... when you love someone? My head hurt.

"Since we're on the subject of families, I've been meaning to ask you... did you finally make up with your sister? She was really upset that night at your house."

"I've tried," I said dully, "but she's not ready to accept my apology."

"It's obvious she idolizes you." Geena said briskly. "She'll come around when she thinks you suffered enough."

"Is that how it works in your house?" I tried picturing what her sixteen-year-old sister, the owner of so many of the cool things Geena wore, could possibly have to apologize for. "Your big sister says she's sorry and you make her sweat it out?"

"No Sloane, that's not how it works in my house."

No one spoke for what felt like a long time. I rubbed my eyes. Stupid me, assuming that all of a sudden we were close enough for me to say anything on my mind. Then Geena began.

"Listen, I'm going to tell you something no one else knows, no one," she blurted out. "but you have to promise..."

"I promise."

"Whatever I ever said in school about my sister is a lie. Marissa is autistic… do you know what that means?

Before I could answer, her words rushed out.

"I mean she's not out of control like she when she was younger. Her screaming fits have just about stopped… and we can go out in public without creating a scene… but my sister is autistic."

"Oh, Geena, I'm so sorry." God, I hoped that was the right thing to say.

"Until last year, she would come into my room and throw all my clothes on the floor and mess with my computer. That was hard. Having her therapy, her doctors, her medications, constantly be the one topic of conversation when I was growing up, that was hard. And never being able to tell her a joke she gets, that's still hard. But today, we're actually in a better place.

"She's an incredible memorizer so she teaches me the words to every JT song the minute it comes out. She loves when we go shopping, as long as I don't make her try on jeans…she hates putting on anything that feels tight. And since she'll only wear the colors pink and purple it's challenging… but not impossible." Incredibly Geena sounded like she was smiling.

My grandmother once said that if everyone put all their problems in a box out on the front porch and then was given a chance to choose any box in the neighborhood to bring home, they'd wind up picking up their own. She might be right.

"It sounds like Marissa is lucky to have you as a sister." I said. "I should take some lessons."

"Seriously? Are you nuts? We all have our stuff to deal with. You'll be fine. You're a much nicer person than I am, you know that." Then she stopped short. "Just ask Molly," she laughed.

It wasn't really funny but it probably was true so I laughed too.

"You see we're friends for a reason," Geena said before we hung up. "We know how to make each other laugh. I'm really glad you called."

I was too. Did it make me a bad person if hearing about Geena's sister actually made me feel better? No. Listening to Geena helped me to see the big picture. It made me realize how the little pity party I was hosting kept me from moving forward.

I stood up, walked into the bathroom and washed my face. When I looked in the mirror, I knew what I had to do next. I propped up my pillows, laid back and dialed Molly's number.

"I probably don't deserve a friend like you." I started as soon as she picked up. "However mad you are at me, please, please don't hang up."

"Thank God," Molly sighed.

Thank God I thought as the blood returned to my fingers.

"If you remember, you're the one who just about kicked me out of your house the last time we spoke," she continued. "I hated to admit the possibility you'd learned to live without me."

My shoulders left my ears.

"The thing was, you were totally right," I began.

"Stop right there," Molly commanded. "That conversation's for a different time. I don't want to talk about that now." She paused. "I've been really worried about you. My mom heard that things aren't going so great with your dad. You never eat lunch any more. You never smile. And you walk around school like a zombie, hardly saying a word to anyone."

"There's nothing happening I want to talk about. It's all so hard."

Molly sighed.

"He might die," I suddenly blurted out. "The doctors are worried that he's not coming back to himself."

"I know," Molly said quietly.

"And what if it's because he went out in the cold and got the flu? Or because I added so much stress to his life that he had a relapse?" I exhaled loudly. "Or because I embarrassed him so and he's afraid I'm going to tell everyone…"

"Whoa, whoa," Molly interrupted. "You embarrassed him so he wants to die? Your father? Not a chance. And leukemia's not a cold. You don't relapse because of a chill."

"You can't know that for sure."

"Sloane, you're a very strong person, but you're not as powerful as you think you are. Your father was in remission. He wasn't cured. I don't know why the cancer came back, but it wasn't because of anything you did."

"What if he dies before we get a chance to talk about all this?" I whispered. "And what if I messed up so bad with Emma that she'll never forget what I did?"

"And what if you tell them both what you're afraid of? The only way what you fear the most could come true is if you do nothing." Then softly Molly added, "I'm sorry. The last thing you need is me being all bossy again."

"Don't apologize. You're so right. It's just that if I talk about it, I'd have to think about it." I swallowed hard. "And if I hurt your feelings because of Geena..."

"You were right." Molly interrupted me. "I was jealous. And that wasn't fair. You're allowed to have more than one friend."

We were both quiet for a moment.

"I don't know how yet, but I promise you I will explain to Emma why I've been so nuts...and my dad... as soon as he's better, I'm going to make him understand that finding out about my biological father has nothing to do with how much I love him."

"If you were here right now I'd give you a hug," Molly said. "You don't know how much I've missed my best friend."

CHAPTER THIRTEEN

It took Dad another seventeen days to raise his blood count high enough to leave the hospital. We took him home with a list of "no's" that was longer than the huge sign at Jones Beach. He couldn't be in crowds or near young children or pets or walk near a construction site. Every rule of good nutrition was reversed. No fresh fruits. No fresh vegetables. Nothing cooked rare. There were plenty of suggestions for the things he could do…just none that appealed to him.

Instead of getting dressed every morning and, as the doctor suggested, taking a walk to build up his strength, he sat around all day in his bathrobe. Nothing we said or did could make his smile reappear. He didn't read his mail or return phone calls. He refused to watch any of his favorite Bill Murray movies Mom got from Netflix. He never even touched the homemade chocolate chip cookies Gram Fed-Xed from Florida. It was as if he was allergic to anything pleasurable.

Even Emma couldn't cheer him up. She'd try to cuddle with him after dinner while he watched the news, but he'd gently ask her to sit at the other end of the couch.

"I don't think it's smart for us to sit so close, honey," he'd say. "You're exposed to thousands of germs a day in third grade. Let's wait a few more weeks."

"The doctor said no kissing on the lips but not no hugging," she'd answer him. "Can't I just lean on you a little?"

"Please, Emma," he'd reply, this time with an edge in his voice. "I'll know when it's time to start hugging again."

I couldn't tell if he remembered what happened between us. Given how little emotion he showed about anything, it was possible he did… and couldn't care less. When he didn't bother to ask about what college teams his graduating seniors would play for next year, we knew we faced a problem of major proportions.

Re-entry into the world after being so close to dying can be tough, the doctors explained. Depression was common. They told Mom how important it was that he regain his strength slowly and try not to dwell on his fears. It was our job to start him moving, keep him active and encourage him until he felt comfortable being out and about.

The doctor suggested group therapy and relaxation exercises, guided imagery tapes and books offering spiritual guidance.

Predictably, Dad scoffed at every idea.

"It's hoogie-moogie, all that stuff. Maybe it works for a certain kind of guy," he scorned, "but whining to a bunch of strangers or picturing myself on a beach in Tahiti is not going to make me feel any better."

"Being so negative won't either." Mom pleaded. "None of these things could hurt. Maybe by getting in touch with…"

"Stop it, Karen," he said angrily. "I'm in touch with more than you'll ever know. Just get off my back."

"Take it easy, Neil," Mom said evenly. "I'm nowhere near your back…yet. But if you don't try to help yourself soon, I'm going to find a reason to climb all over you."

That was as forceful as I ever heard her. Emma looked a little scared. But as far as the object of Mom's comments, he ignored every word.

It was 3:30 the next Wednesday, one of the rare days I came straight home after school. Dad was watching some old black and white war movie. Emma was playing at a friend's house. As I opened the refrigerator and poured myself a glass of milk, I noticed an article ripped out of a magazine, entitled *Writing Unsent Letters Can Heal,* circled in red on the kitchen counter. "Just think about it," Mom's neat handwriting begged in red Magic Marker across the top of the page. She was always leaving him inspirational quotes or funny jokes, in the hope one might raise his spirits.

"Writing an unsent letter can help provide emotional healing and personal growth," the first sentence promised. "It affords you the opportunity to express everything from pain to rage, without fear of reprisal. Write to a person beyond your voice's reach to work out the emotional kinks in your life. Write to a person you feel has wronged you, who you find you have trouble speaking to in person, or maybe even someone you have never met. Whether you're venting or confessing or figuring out a problem, write honestly without hesitation… no one is going to read what you write."

Suddenly I felt flushed. I should write one of these letters. *Dear donor dad.* The very thought sent my knee jumping up and down. Just then the phone rang.

"What are you doing? Can you come over now? I have a surprise I have to show you right away," Geena squealed.

A surprise? To show me?

"I need you to see it today. And I can't bring it to school. I'm home with my sister, otherwise I'd come to you."

"OK, I'll be right there," I said, not sorry at all to have a reason to leave the oppressive sadness of my house.

I yelled out to my dad that I was going to a friend to practice our dance and ran the ten blocks to Geena's house in record time. I rang the bell, trying to catch my breath. A second later I knocked. After what seemed an eternity, I rang the bell again. I heard someone inside yell, "Hang on, will you? I'll be right there."

My red face flushed even more. I obviously misjudged how long I was waiting and annoyed someone inside. Ugh.

The door opened and there stood Geena's mother.

"Hello," she said, extending her bracelet-laden arm to shake my hand.

I put my hand out to meet hers and wound up staring at her

breasts which looked about ready to speak. "Help" they would say if they could, "get us out of this teeny tank top. It's mortifying being covered by *I'm so bad, I'm good.*"

She had a little bag draped on her shoulder and car keys in her hand. Between her fingers and toes and lips and cheeks, there was a whole lot of hot pink going on. She had bangs down to her eyebrows and her straight extremely blonde hair reached the middle of her back. If you squinted just a bit she could pass for one of the high school cheerleaders.

"I'm Marlee," she said, raising her chin as she carefully assessed my appearance from head to toe. Just then, Geena came up behind her. She gave me a hug, grabbed my hand and pulled me up the stairs.

"Sorry Mom, we're in a hurry," she said. "We have a program to watch that starts in five minutes."

"No problem, darling," Marlee answered. She sounded sarcastic and pleasant at the same time. "Just keep an eye on your sister. She's had a rough day."

"Is that why you're running out of the house… because she had a rough day?" Geena muttered under her breath. But her mother was already gone.

"So now that you've met the blonde Kardashian," grinned Geena, "come meet my sister.

More than a little nervous, I followed her, not sure what to expect.

"Wait till you see her room," she whispered as we walked upstairs and down the hallway to a closed bedroom door. "She loves to collect things."

"I want you to meet my friend Sloane," she announced, opening the door slowly after getting no response to her knock.

There in the center of bizarrely organized chaos sat Marissa. She was surrounded on the rug by what looked like dozens of stuffed sheep. On the wall behind her were three shelves filled with at least a hundred Webkinz animals meticulously arranged in alphabetical order, from Afghan hound to Zircon puppy. They looked so perfect, like everything was on sale. If Emma ever saw this room, her head would explode.

"I want you to meet my friend Sloane," Geena repeated.

Marissa continued playing with her sheep as if she hadn't heard a word.

"Don't feel bad," Geena said under her breath, "she prefers her animals' company to anyone else's."

"Come on Marissa, say hi to my friend. Eyes up, remember? Look in my eyes, then say hi."

For a fleeting second, we made eye contact.

"Hi Sloane," she intoned before returning her attention back to the sheep.

"Hi Marissa," I said, trying to sound relaxed. "Your animals are amazing."

"They're sheep."

"Well then, your sheep are amazing." I looked at Geena. She raised her eyebrows and nodded, encouraging me to continue.

"Do they each have a name?"

Marissa looked directly at me with no expression.

"Of course they each have a name. Do you want to know what they are?"

"Sure."

Geena opened her mouth, then hesitated. "This might take a while," she said, rolling her eyes.

"Well, this is Puffkins," Marissa began, pointing to the black and white sheep she was holding. "This guy is Fernando Fernadez. My father bought him for me. That's Shaun the Sheep. He likes to sit next to his girlfriend. Her name is Lamby. Her baby is that little one, Ewey. Next to him is Sheepy, I got her when I was five. Shep looks like an old English sheep dog but he's not. He's a sheep. Baba is from England. My aunt brought her back for me. Wanna touch her? She's the softest one of all."

I bent down and nuzzled her ear. "Mmmmm, she is soft," I agreed. "Is she your favorite?"

Marissa nodded. "She comes to school with me every day. And out to dinner. And to the doctor." She gently tugged the sheep away from me. "Actually she's with me at all times. Do you like Justin Timberlake?" she asked as she returned Baba to her place in the circle.

Yes, I do." I smiled.

I was about to tell her his new album was coming out next week but she went on.

"Is your birthday in September? Mine is. The 21st. I'm a Virgo. Geena's is in November. The 12th. She's a Scorpio."

This time I waited before replying.

"If you want to know the names of my other animals," she continued, turning to the shelves behind her, "I'll tell you."

Geena touched my shoulder before I could respond.

"Next time, Marissa. Sloane and I have to watch a television show in my room now, OK?"

"OK," Marissa shrugged. "But can we read later?"

"Sure. I think we're up to chapter eight, right?"

"Right."

"We're reading *The Fault In Our Stars* together," Geena explained as she shut the door behind her. "I'm loving it a lot more than she is but she knows all the kids in school are into it so we take turns reading it out loud before bed."

"Uh huh," I said, as if watching too-pretty, too-popular, too-self-centered Geena morphing into Mother Teresa didn't completely blow my mind. I was glad she couldn't see my face as I followed her into her bedroom.

"You did great in there, by the way. She likes you."

"No problem," I said sincerely.

"I owe you one." Geena suddenly looked uncomfortable. "Can I ask you not to tell anyone… I mean it's not exactly a secret but most of the kids don't know…"

I just looked at her.

"Real friends understand… they don't judge…and I don't have many real friends."

"How can you say that?" I said, thinking of at least a dozen girls who would do anything to trade places with me this very second.

"Most of the girls in school only suck up to me because I'm popular. They don't really like me… You didn't, remember?"

Her words hung in the air. So in exchange for a reputation of having everything and everyone under control, all she had to give up was revealing any chinks in the armor, anything about herself that was less than beautiful. As if she read my thoughts, the queen quickly regained her throne. "Listen, don't feel bad. Trust me, it's fine being the hottest girl in the grade, really it is."

Luckily just then we arrived at Geena's bedroom. In the center of the closed door was a small privacy doorbell. That was cool.

I looked around at the royal residence. On either side of her bed were two pink lamps wrapped top to bottom with black feather boas. A leg doing a high kick in fishnet stockings and a strawberry colored garter protruded from one wall. The other wall had posters of Beyonce and Rihanna. Instead of my plain white dressers, Geena's clothes nestled in shiny neon lockers. On her desk sat her computer, hidden under a fake fur cover. And finally there was a makeup mirror with lights all around it like you see backstage in the movies, next to a stand displaying at least a dozen fabulous glittery headbands in all colors.

"So, how are things in your house?" asked Geena, now on her knees and searching carefully through her bottom drawer.

"I'm not sure," I sighed. "The more time that goes by, the more sure I thought I'd be about what to do next. About everything. But that's not happening."

"Well, lucky for you, what's going to happen next is going to make you feel so much better," Geena bubbled.

I was pretty sure she didn't even hear what I said.

"Just close your eyes."

I was so not in the mood to pretend to feel better but I closed my eyes, listening to what sounded like Geena changing her clothes.

"Ta-da, OK, you can look now."

I opened my eyes.

"You are looking at an award winning costume for our dance!" she exclaimed. "No offense but when it comes to clothes, I knew you'd trust my taste!"

Geena was wearing a scarily skimpy shiny black top with white graffiti that barely covered her chest and a pair of really low black pants.

Could my life get any worse?

How could I convince anyone our music is not bragging about degrading women if we wore that outfit? I blinked twice, praying that the top would magically grow fabric.

"You really can't see the full effect," she prattled on. "I asked Mr. Altman if we could be lit with a black light. But don't worry; I didn't take all the credit, if that's what you're thinking... I told him we both saw it on a video and decided it would be perfect for our dance." She tugged at the waistband of her pants, pulling them an inch further down. "You won't believe how sick this printing looks under a black light. It's almost fluorescent."

She went to Mr. Altman and asked him about the lights? *She* told him I approved of the idea? I'll bet she didn't show him that teeny top. We'd never be allowed to dance in something that showed so much skin.

"And of course I didn't show him what we were going to wear," she laughed. "He would freak, don't you think?"

"Yeah, he'd freak," I said slowly. "Do you really think it's smart to wear something so against the rules at a school competition?"

"Like the audience won't think it's beyond fabulous," Geena scoffed. "He'll hear their reaction and change his mind, you'll see."

"You already bought four of them?" I asked, my heart sinking.

"They were sooo cheap, on sale at H & M... I couldn't resist. Don't you love them?"

When I hesitated, Geena said, "Don't worry about the price. My dad never checks the credit card he gave me... I already decided since I took responsibility for the decision, I would pay for them."

"It's not the price," I stammered, "I'm just surprised you..."

"Oh, it's OK," Geena said warmly. "I told you I owed you one. You've worked so hard on this show. And as far as Mr. Altman goes, leave him to me. It'll be fine. When the seventh grade pulls an upset and wins first place for the first time in history, it'll be worth it, you'll see."

Geena was so entranced with her reflection in the mirror she never realized I hadn't said one word about the costume.

At midnight I sat in my bedroom in front of a blank computer screen. My mind ricocheted from one maddening problem to the next. How will I ever to be able to tell Molly about Geena's costumes? How long will it be before I'll be able to talk normally with my dad? How will I find the words to explain to Emma why I acted like such a jerk? Uncomfortably full from swallowing too many secrets, suddenly the idea of writing one of those unsent letters didn't seem so bizarre. At the least, it might free up some space in my head to resolve a few real life problems. Yeah, maybe the whole idea was ridiculous, but no more so than the rest of my life.

Dear donor dad,

Calling you that sounds less important and less intimidating than biological father …and although it's kind of cold, it's kind of perfect for your contribution of frozen ingredients. First know that whether you are a symphony conductor or a guy who does odd jobs and lives in a trailer, I want nothing from you. While yes, it would be interesting to know what religion you are and what makes you laugh, I'd never want to hurt my dad by actually meeting you. A photo would be nice… and maybe a little information on your parents… just in case there's some inherited health stuff I should know.

I thought if I ever got the chance to communicate with you, there would be loads of things I'd want to tell you about who I am… what my life is like, my grades and my hobbies… but now that I'm actually writing to you, I realize you probably don't care… and strangely that's OK with me. I have my own family and hopefully you have yours.

When I first found out a few months ago I was a "cryokid," I thought there was something mysterious and almost magical about our genetic relationship. And because I really couldn't talk about it with anyone, I felt embarrassed for being so curious about you. I was upset because if I were adopted, I would've been told and could probably trace my birth parents. But now I understand that under their circumstances at the time, my mom and dad found their own best way to make a child.

So if I think about what I hope to get out of writing this letter, it's this. I choose to believe you donated sperm for the right reasons, not just for the money. You are not a nasty secret to be buried and forgotten but a reason to be grateful. There would be no me without you, and for that I owe you big. Thanks for listening.

Sloane Davis

I reread what I wrote and didn't change a word. Instead, I saved it and closed the light. As I got into bed, I yawned loudly. It was a surprise how short the letter was. It was a surprise realizing I wasn't nearly as passionately involved with this man as I thought. And best of all, considering all the fires I had yet to put out, it was a surprise how quickly I fell into the best night's sleep I'd had in weeks.

Chapter Fourteen

"Those are cool sneakers, are they new?" I asked Emma the next afternoon after school. Dad was taking a nap, leaving the two of us alone in the kitchen.

"They're about two months old," she answered cautiously. "Does that make them new, still?"

"The way you take care of your things, it does," I said. "After two months, my sneakers look like I've had them two years."

"I can't help it if I'm careful," Emma replied defensively. "I like it when they're very, very white."

"Hey, I'm not criticizing you," I explained. "I was just stating a fact. It's a good thing to take pride in your things. I wish I were a little more like you that way."

Since the show, Emma was on her guard, almost flinching every time I tried to say something nice. It made me sick to think I made her react that way. If she were older, I could tell her the truth, that I acted so mean because I hated the idea of her being Mom and Dad's real child. I'd tell her how much I wanted Dad to be as proud of me as he was of her.

But at eight years old, she had no knowledge of conception, natural or techno. Even if she got through the technical part, which she never would, she was way too young to understand how much I envied her sturdy limb on the family tree.

"You want some chocolate milk?" I offered. "Mom's got shortbread cookies."

"Sure." Then five seconds later, "Why are you being so nice to me?"

"I only offered to pour some milk in a glass," I said lightly. "No big deal."

She watched me stir in Fox's U-Bet chocolate syrup.

"Can I lick the spoon?" she asked.

"Uh-huh." I put the spoon back in the jar and filled it half way with the thick syrup. "Here," I said, carefully handing it over to her so it didn't drip all over the counter.

"Mmmm," she started to hum as she licked the spoon. Then she froze mid-mmm when she saw me watching.

"What's wrong?"

"You hate it when I make noises when I eat."

"You're not eating. Make as much noise as you want," I said, turning away as I screwed the cap on the jar. A single tear fell on the counter.

"So, how's school?" I asked, clearing my throat. I took a seat at the kitchen table. "Are you still a celebrity? After that article in the paper, did any kids ask for your autograph?"

Emma looked at me warily.

"I'm just trying to make conversation, Emma," I said carefully. "I really want to know. Did Miss Klein make a big fuss when you got back to school?"

"Why," Emma said slowly, "do you want to know all of a sudden? You never once asked me anything about school before."

She got me. I never did ask her about school because most of the time I heard too much about her day at dinner. But lately dinner had become such a somber occasion, she hadn't been talking much.

"Well, maybe I'm changing. People go through stages as they grow." I took a deep breath. I had to take advantage of this opportunity. I had no idea how I was going to get her to understand my apology… let alone accept it…but I owed her to try. "For a while there I was pretty evil, pretty nasty to be around."

Emma nodded.

"I acted that way because I wasn't happy. I know now that's no excuse for being mean. I was angry at other things in my life and I took it out on you. If I weren't such a coward I would've talked to the person who made me upset. Instead I picked on you and I hate myself for it. I'm really sorry."

I searched Emma's face for a reaction but she just sat there. This wasn't going to be easy.

"Can I have more U-Bet?" she asked in a strong voice, holding up her clean spoon.

I took the spoon and reopened the jar. "OK, but don't tell Mom." This time I filled the spoon and walked slowly back to where she was sitting.

"That spoon was in my mouth already. You should have gotten a new one out of the drawer. Mom said you're never supposed to put your spoon back because of all the bacteria in your mouth."

"It's different with chocolate syrup," I bluffed. "The cocoa beans kill any germs instantly."

Emma looked confused. She was pretty sure I'd made that up but she couldn't be certain.

She took the spoon from my hand and just stared at it. Then she carefully put it in her glass. Instead of stirring she looked up at me and asked, "Promise you won't go getting all mad again if I ask you something?" Her gaze was strong but her voice wavered slightly.

"I promise."

"Why didn't you come see my show?" The room was very still. She looked away and gave all her attention to the task of slowly mixing the inch full of milk left with a heaping teaspoon of U-Bet.

I didn't answer right away.

"Why didn't you come?" she repeated, louder this time, willing me to look at her face as I searched for the right words.

I couldn't believe how nervous I felt. There was nothing to do but tell the truth, watered down, of course.

"I was jealous. I know that sounds dumb, I'm twelve and you're eight, but I was. I couldn't stand seeing Mom and Dad make a big fuss over you one more time. You don't realize it but it feels like that's all I ever do...watch them enjoying how cute you are. But if I had any idea they weren't there, I swear Emma, I would've been there." I stopped to capture her gaze. "I think about that night all the time. I never meant to hurt you."

"That's the stupidest thing. Being jealous of a third-grader. You're in the middle school. You wear lip gloss. You have a cell phone." Emma folded her arms across her chest. "No, really, Sloane. Tell me the truth. Why didn't you come to my show?"

She looked so solemn. I never anticipated she wouldn't believe me.

"Emma, I swear on my life, that's the truth. Why would I make up a story where I look like such a loser? Everyone knows you're the attention grabber in the family. You're funny. You're a great athlete. You're a terrific actress. And sometimes it's hard for me to get my share."

Emma blinked. "But you're so beautiful."

I felt a lump in my throat.

"And you get A's all the time. Daddy's always telling me I should see how hard you work because soon it's not going to be so easy for me to be the best swimmer. And I'm going to have to work harder like you."

I cleared my throat. "Well, that's something I never knew. You see what happens when families don't tell each other how they really feel?"

Emma looked at me blankly. I was pushing it. A kid who's reading *Amelia Bedelia* wasn't exactly ready to discuss the dynamics involved in the breakdown of family communications.

"Whatever," she said, shrugging off my question. "Can I ask you one more thing?" She was sitting on her knees now with her hands clasped on the table.

"Shoot."

"You just said that people change. Like when you got so mean and angry at everybody." She bit her lip. "You're not going to change back to be like that again, are you?"

"No, Emma, I promise. I won't." I said softly. "It's not just for your sake that I'm saying that. I don't ever want to feel so crummy again."

"And what about Daddy?"

"What about him?"

"Is he going to change back to the way he was too? He's not nasty, he's just so bloopy all the time."

I smiled at the perfect word she chose to describe Dad's behavior.

"If he has my bone marrow and he's better," she went on, "why is he still acting like he's sick?"

"He's not all better yet, Emma. He's getting better but it takes time. As his strength comes back, you'll see, that bloopiness will slowly disappear."

I prayed I was right.

"How come you and Daddy changed and Mommy and I didn't? Does that mean I take after Mommy and you take after Daddy?"

"Well, if you mean are you and Mommy more sensitive to other people's feelings and less moody than Dad and I...probably yes."

Emma shook her head thoughtfully. "It's good it's even then, right? Two and two."

I smiled as I walked over and gave her a hug. "Yes, it's good."

Chapter Fifteen

"So the show is Friday night. When am I going to see what you guys are wearing?" Mr. Altman asked.

My heart pounded like a small animal trapped in an airless cage.

"Stop looking like you killed somebody." whispered Geena. "It told you I'll take care of this."

"My mom picked up the shirts we ordered… and the dumb salesgirl gave her the wrong sizes," Geena explained. "She's going back to return them this afternoon."

"All right, as long as you have them for the run through tomorrow night," Mr. Altman said.

"No problem," Geena smiled. "They'll be here."

I wondered what lie she'd come up with tomorrow. Or whether she'd spend a minute worrying about it.

"Haven't you seen what we're wearing?" Molly asked. "How could you let her make such an important decision alone?" She was frowning. "I hope they're flattering on all of us, not just her."

"I saw them," I answered flatly.

"So what do they look like?"

"You'll see them tomorrow," I mumbled. "They're hard to describe…"

Molly looked into my eyes, then pursed her lips.

"Please, can't we just rehearse right now? It won't make any difference what we wear if we screw up the dance."

Molly shook her head but got into position on stage.

"Bend your knees...thrust your chest out...rotate your arms in time with your chest movements... I directed. "Knee lift to the count of three, come on let's go."

Those who think hip-hop is about being lazy or mediocre or comfortable should have seen us that afternoon. We each accepted the challenge to be perfect, the same way a gymnast would. I wished my father understood the effort it took to look effortless.

"Good work girls," I said breathlessly at the end of our two-hour practice. "You nailed it the last time around."

"I'm so excited to see our costumes," Rebecca squealed as she grabbed a towel. "I heard they're really hot."

"Mmmm" I said as I bent over to tie my shoes.

"I hope Geena's mom doesn't have any trouble getting us the right sizes. That would be a bummer at the last minute."

Not as much of a bummer as the fact that I am your dance captain, I thought. I am responsible for what we look like on stage. This was going to be a disaster. And it was all on me.

———

"So here's the deal," Geena whispered at the dress rehearsal the next night. She bent over and motioned for us to join her, knee level. The four of us were sitting on a bench, preparing to change into our costumes. She pulled four white tee shirts out of a shopping bag, then the tiny white and black graffiti tank tops I'd seen. "For tonight we'll wear these shirts underneath. I'll collect them when we're finished and conveniently forget to bring them back tomorrow." She looked delighted with her plan to get over Mr. Altman's objections.

"I picked up these pink neon scarves too. Rebecca, you wear it on your arm, Sloane, you wear yours across your forehead, and Molly, you wear yours around your neck. I'll tie mine around my ponytail.

Molly looked at right me.

"You knew about this?" She held up the graffiti top and shook her head. "This wouldn't fit Emma. My mother's going to kill me." Molly threw the shirt on the bench. She stood up, putting her hands on her waist. "Our dance is good enough to win without a cheesy costume, don't you think?"

Geena's eyes narrowed. She looked at me, then Rebecca, but both of us avoided her gaze.

"Oooh, Mommy will be mad...." she mocked.

No one said a word as we got dressed. The tank barely squeezed on over our tee shirts. When we heard Mr. Altman introduce us, we ran to our places in the middle of the stage and waited for the music to start.

A guy in the back of the auditorium yelled, "You the girls who wanted the black light?"

"Yes," Geena yelled back. "Let us know how it looks."

The music began. Robotically we ran through the short broken steps. It was the first time in my life my mind kept working while I danced. I forced myself to focus as one combination connected with the next, then repeated, then got reintroduced slower than before. My bra cut into my armpit, reminding me with every move what a coward I was. There was no joy in my performance and it was a miracle I hadn't messed up.

"Good idea," Mr. Altman nodded from his seat in the front row. "about the lights. They add real energy."

Geena beamed and curtseyed.

"Are you girls comfortable in those shirts? They looked a little small. Maybe your mom should have bought them in a bigger size."

"Nah, we're good, right girls?"

No one answered her.

"My one suggestion would be to add a few smiles tomorrow night. Your technique is fine but what happened to your passion? Have fun up there. That's how you'll connect with your audience."

"No problem," Geena said gaily as we walked off the stage.

Speak for yourself, I thought. We got dressed quietly, surrounded by the eighth and ninth graders chattering away excitedly as they awaited their turn. Out of the corner of my eye, I noticed Geena shoving the four tee shirts into her dance bag.

"Don't worry," said the eighth grade dance captain, mistaking my slouched shoulders for disappointment in the way we performed. "I'm sure you'll be ten times better tomorrow."

"Thanks," I said, "I hope you're right."

I let the phone ring and ring when I got home...four calls from Molly. If I didn't have the courage to stand up to Geena and tell her how I felt about our outfits, I certainly didn't have the guts to face talking to Molly.

The next night I left the house really early, refusing my mother's ride to school. That she and Emma would be in the audience made a bad situation even more miserable. I could imagine their faces when we came onstage.

Molly was the first to arrive.

"Look," she began, "I don't want to cause any trouble. You're the dance captain and if you say we should wear that slutty costume, I'll wear it. But look at your face. You know how wrong it is. You hate it as much as I do. I just don't get why you let Geena take over."

I shrugged, envying Molly for not being susceptible to Geena's aura. She was lucky... or maybe she just had a backbone.

"Geena knows more about what looks good than we do. Maybe they're not as bad as we think."

Molly looked like she felt sorry for me.

"Anyway, it's too late now."

The room began to fill. Geena and Rebecca came in together. Geena pulled out a lipstick from her cosmetic bag.

"It's Rock Star Red," she squealed. "Let's all wear it."

Then she handed us each our tiny tanks. We pulled them over our heads, then tied on our bandanas. I took a deep breath and walked over to the mirror. The top was pulled tight across my chest... and really short, exposing my whole stomach. I glanced at the others. Rebecca and I shrugged at the same instant, exchanging a look that said we both felt the same way. Molly looked the most upset but she didn't say anything. Geena, however, was ecstatic.

"Ohmigod," she exclaimed. "We are the bomb. We're going to win, I know it!"

The older girls just stared.

"How do you expect to get away with that?" one asked, looking directly at our belly buttons.

"Watch us," Geena retorted.

They did. They watched when the audience murmured as the black light highlighted our costume. They watched as we danced better than we ever did. And they watched at the end of the night, with all three grades on stage awaiting the winner, as Mr. Altman disqualified us in front of the whole school for disregarding the dress regulations.

It's funny what you remember about a moment like that. Time freezes. I found Emma in the audience and will never forget how sad her eyes were as she looked at me. My mother had her hand over her mouth. And my father... my father came!... and stared ahead grimly, his arms folded across his chest.

The curtains closed and we made our way backstage with the other performers.

"What a jerk," Geena said. Her voice was high pitched and shrill. "I can't believe he did that."

"What can't you believe?" yelled out someone behind us. "That you dressed like skanks and you got called on it?" A few kids laughed.

Geena recoiled like she'd been slapped.

"They're right, you know." I said quietly, suddenly too tired to keep on pretending.

Geena stopped walking. "Oh really," she said, "do tell."

"I messed up. I didn't have the courage to say no to you. Those shirts were a terrible idea and I went along with it."

Rebecca and Molly looked at each other.

"What are you talking about?" Geena said, blinking as she pushed back her hair. "This whole dance would have sucked without me. I helped with the..."

"No Geena, we lost because of the outfits you picked out," I interrupted. "Otherwise we might have won." I felt no pressure to return her gaze. "Don't worry though, no one is going to blame you. It's my fault. I'm taking responsibility.

Geena looked around to find an ally, the color falling from her face.

"Rebecca, do you hear her? I guess Sloane feels she doesn't need friends any more."

Rebecca stared back, expressionless.

"I have friends, real ones, and you know that," my voice cracked. "I thought you were one of them. But I can't always be afraid to tell you the truth because I'm scared you'll get mad at me." I was sweating and my heart was pounding but for once not in a bad way.

Rebecca and Molly didn't move a muscle.

"I'd end this conversation now, if I were you," Geena lashed out. Her eyes were blinking double-time, like mine sometimes do when I'm trying hard to hold back tears.

"And if I were you, I'd be ashamed for not admitting I made a mistake," I advised. "It's not that hard to apologize when you're wrong. You should try it sometime."

I walked away feeling unreasonably good after such a disastrous night.

CHAPTER SIXTEEN

I walked home from school inhaling a beautiful May afternoon that promised the arrival of the best six months of the year. The sky was achingly blue and nearly cloudless as I once more reviewed the fallout from last night's events.

"You made an error in judgment... and you were penalized for it," Dad had said. "End of discussion."

Incredibly, Mom apologized for being so preoccupied with everything going on that she never even asked about what we were going to wear. She knew I'd never choose those outfits and just said she hoped next time I would trust my own instincts.

I was full of gratitude knowing they understood no one could feel worse about our getting eliminated than I did.

At lunchtime I knocked on Mr. Altman's door. I heard chairs scraping as whoever was sitting in his office, stood up...then voices as they moved towards the door. I stepped back as the door opened and Geena walked out.

Was it a good thing or not that she beat me to Mr. Altman's office? I was so unnerved I didn't know how to react. Luckily I wasn't alone.

"Oh, hi," Geena faltered. Then she just stood there in the doorway. Her cheeks were flushed and she wouldn't look at me. She didn't appear tearful but there was a balled up tissue in her fist. And still she didn't move.

"How's Marissa doing?" That's what came out of my mouth. Without me having any conscious input. Not bad. It reminded Geena that once upon a time she trusted me. And it had nothing to do with why we were both standing in Mr. Altman's office.

"Good, actually." She paused. "She finally let me iron her hair and she looks amazing."

I knew it bothered Geena that Marissa's long, glossy black hair was always messy, pulled back in a low ponytail. She'd never let anyone touch it.

"She didn't come last night," Geena went on, "because we thought the music would be too loud for her."

I nodded.

"Anyway," she laughed nervously, "last night it was finally my turn to have a meltdown."

That was a loaded statement. I looked directly into her eyes. She returned my gaze, then turned away.

Geena swallowed hard. "And how is your sister? I noticed her in the audience last night. Does that mean things are better between you guys?"

Wait a minute. Really? This was how it was going to go?

"Getting there," I answered her honestly. "We're talking at least. It's going to take a while." I remembered how Emma actually clapped last night when I described my exchange with Geena. This was so weird.

"Can you girls continue this conversation later on?" Mr. Altman asked. "I have a class in fifteen minutes."

"Of course," we both said at exactly the same time. Then we laughed. Then we felt super awkward.

"I'll call you, all right?" Geena asked almost timidly.

"Sure," I said as she rushed off.

Mr. Altman closed the door behind me. He took his seat behind the desk, interlaced his fingers behind his neck and stretched out his feet. Clearly the ball was in my court.

"OK," I said hurriedly, "I don't know what you just heard but I'm not going to blame what happened on anyone else. I just want you to know how sorry I am that we kept you in the dark about those costumes. It's my fault. I was the captain. Because I didn't have the nerve to stand up to Geena, I know I forced you to eliminate us."

Mr. Altman looked very serious.

"I promise you nothing like this will ever happen again."

"Good," he said. "I believe that." He straightened up in the chair and leaned forward, clasping his hands on his desk. "Look," he said quietly, "I know how hard you girls worked. I told you how much I loved your routine. But choosing that outfit was just plain stupid."

"Believe me, I know," I said, lowering my eyes.

"I just had this identical conversation with Geena. I told her that if she had enough confidence in her dancing, she wouldn't need to resort to dressing so inappropriately."

Confidence? Geena lacked confidence?

"You know Sloane, there were a lot of things I didn't like about myself when I was your age... but for the most part, I was pretty happy to be me. I never found anyone I wanted to trade places with. Not the handsomest, the smartest, or the best athlete... I see that same sensibility in you."

It was true. As awful as the last few months have been I never would exchange my life... my crazy family... for anyone else's. Certainly not Geena's.

"I am not excusing either of you for what happened last night. I just want you to understand that who you see as top-of-the-heap, most popular Geena, worries a lot more about what other people think of her than you ever will."

I shook my head.

"When you get right down to it, she thought your performance needed more of an edge. You knew it didn't. She was the one who was scared to lose, you were the one with the faith that your best was good enough."

Obviously Geena admitted the costumes were her idea. And Mr. Altman was asking me to kind of forgive her. This was so not what I expected.

"All right then," he smiled, "we're done here. Your apology is accepted. I hope you won't let this keep you from trying out for dance captain next year."

"It won't," I smiled. I was about to thank him for being the most amazing teacher ever but he waved me out of his office. "Go, go. Today is my first day without a show to worry about. I deserve a little peace."

103

As I approached the corner, the light turned green. I walked a bit quicker. The moment I stepped down off the curb, I heard a honk. There, three cars down, waved my mom. She leaned over to open the passenger door to let me in.

"Surprise," she said. "Want to go for some ice cream?"

"Sure," I said, sliding into the car. With Dad around all the time now, it seemed like forever since the two of us had been alone.

"I'm sorry if I scared you," she went on as the car started to move. "You looked like you were a million miles away. Still beating yourself up about last night?"

"Just thinking about everything... and nothing," I sighed.

Mom was quiet. Then she took a deep breath. "So did you ever write that unsent letter?" she asked. Her eyes looked straight ahead; her two hands gripped the steering wheel.

My eyes widened.

Still not looking at me, she allowed herself a small smile. Then it hit me. "You left the article there for *me* to see it?"

She nodded.

Wow. I would've bet my dealing with Mr. X was the furthest thing from her mind.

"I did write one. It was a weird experience," I began slowly, "sitting down and trying to have an actual conversation with... the guy. For months all I thought about was getting in touch with him, and then when I sort of pretended I did, I couldn't believe I didn't have that much to say."

"Well, we thought it was worth a shot. We hoped you might get some clarity or closure...."

"We?"

"Yes. Actually it was your father's idea. The doctor sent him the article but he thought it might be helpful for you. He had me write on it and leave it out on the counter for you to find."

My father? My dad wanted me to contact my sperm donor?

"Mom," I pleaded, "if we're going to talk about this, could you please at least pull over?"

When we reached the next corner, she swung into the shopping center and parked way at the far end where there were no other cars.

Then she shut off the engine and turned to face me.

"It took me long enough, but I'm ready," she said calmly. "What do you want to know?"

After all this time you'd think I'd be nervous... or excited... or scared... but suddenly I was calm too. I took a deep breath.

"Weren't you ever curious about the guy whose baby you carried? What did you know about him? How did you choose him?" The words came tumbling out.

"I know you're going to find this hard to believe, Sloane, but all I cared about is that he be young and healthy. If you start asking questions, where do you stop? How are his teeth? Was he a Democrat or Republican? What baseball team does he root for? The more we would know, the more afraid we would be of making the wrong choice."

"So you didn't ask any questions about him? As long as he was healthy, you didn't care about anything else?" My mother looked out the driver's side window.

"My doctor knew me very well. And he knew Dad was having a hard time. I hope this isn't too difficult for you to hear but I never wanted to fill my head with details that would make this phantom person more real. I hated the whole idea of shopping for sperm..."

She turned to me.

"Are you OK?" she asked worriedly.

I nodded.

"My husband, my best friend, my partner in life was going to be your father." She stopped and pushed my bangs out of my eyes. "This man's job was finished before you were born."

My hands felt clammy. "Didn't you ever think that maybe I'd be mad if I found out?" Now it was my turn to look out the window.

"Oh course I thought about it. I worried for years about the day we'd be having this conversation." Mom stopped to search in her bag for a tissue. Then she tugged at my sleeve and pulled me close to her. Never was I more grateful that we owned the only car in the neighborhood without bucket seats in the front. Very quietly she continued, "But I had to believe I would be able to make you understand why we did what we did."

We undid our seatbelts and I lay my head on her chest.

"I convinced myself if I listened hard and heard you, I'd come up with the words to help you absorb it all." She bent down and kissed the top of my head. "I have no shame or misgivings about how you were created and I prayed to God that you would inherit that."

I closed my eyes and just stayed there. Then Mom broke the silence.

"I was inseminated with the sperm of a five foot eleven inch blond man who graduated in 2000 with a Ph.D in chemistry from the University of Pennsylvania."

I could feel her heart beating fast.

"The doctor told me he wrote on his application that he won two major physics awards in his senior year." She waited. "The thought crossed my mind when I heard that, that a person could probably track down that yearbook and see who he was and what he looked like. If one day a person wanted to."

Although physically Dad was in remission, the doctor was concerned about the reasons behind his vacant eyes and shuffling feet. He stopped talking about going back to work. In fact, he practically stopped talking all together. We got used to speaking around him at dinner, almost as if he were deaf or didn't understand the language. Each day we prayed the pilot light deep inside him would re-ignite and he would rejoin us in the land of the living.

Part of me was shocked that the man who crafted the best half time pep talks for ten straight winning seasons seemed so totally unmotivated. Part of me was sad that our family felt broken and unfixable. And part of me was consumed with guilt, sure that my words had contributed mightily to his depression.

On Sunday morning Molly came over. We had made plans to walk over to the bagel store and have breakfast. She hadn't seen my dad for a long time and brought him a present...black and white cookies, his favorite. But he just grunted thanks, barely picking his eyes up from the newspaper.

"How long has it been since your father's transplant?" Molly asked as we made our way down the block.

"Long enough for him to look a lot better than he does."

"It's not how he looks that bothers me…" Molly said. "I guess from how gung ho he's always been, I expected by this time…"

"He'd be working harder to get well," I finished her sentence. My words sounded harsh in the still morning air.

Molly didn't respond.

"He never gave up on anything, not ever… not until I told him I knew about him not being my real father." My voice broke. "Being stripped of your manhood and your entire immune system in the same week can mess with a guy's confidence, don't you think?"

Molly stopped walking.

"What are you talking about?"

"I'm not saying that's the only reason he's not getting better… but I certainly didn't help."

"So if that's what you believe, what are you going to do about it?" Molly asked, her brow furrowed. "You can't just sit around and watch him get weaker and weaker."

"As if anything I say would make him feel better. Seriously, what do you suggest? That I tell him I'm over the shock. That I say, sorry, I over-acted, forget the whole thing? He'd know I'm lying." Suddenly I felt exhausted. "I'm sorry if I'm yelling at you but…"

"But nothing," Molly fired back. "You're acting as helpless as he is. Don't be afraid of his moods. Tell him how angry you are."

I stared at her.

"Your father is still the same strong, stubborn man he always was, only now it's working against him." She stopped. "You have to get him to snap out of it, Sloane."

We walked the rest of the way in silence.

"Oh, by the way, out of the blue, Geena came up to me and said she was sorry about what happened. She said she never gave you a chance to say no and that she had no right to take charge like she did."

That was pretty momentous. Although she never apologized to me, we recently we began exchanging smiles in the hall.

"You could see it took a lot out of her to say she was sorry. I believed her."

I just listened.

"So what I'm saying is, after she spoke to me I thought a lot about what happened. And I decided whether she's being Hannah Montana or Miley Cyrus, it doesn't make her a completely bad person. Or you for wanting to be her friend."

God, I loved Molly.

We got to the bagel store and took our place at the back of a long line.

"Does anyone actually ever order a spinach bagel?" I asked.

"Uh-huh. They also order peanut butter bagels, pumpkin bagels, blueberry bagels...you come up with a ridiculous enough ingredient, they'll bake it in a bagel."

We sat down at one of the tables for two near the counter. The front window was fogged up from the heat of the ovens. Even though it was after the breakfast rush, there was still a line of customers, mostly fathers, accompanied by one or two of their kids. For years my dad and I would be on the same line, bringing back bagels and the paper every Sunday morning. The kids all raced to the door to check out a new red Corvette convertible that pulled up to the curb. I looked carefully at their faces as they admired the car. Except for one easy pair, a dad and his son, both with curly red hair and freckles, it was hard to pair up each man with his family.

"Can you figure out which kid goes with which dad?"

"Not all of 'em...but most of them." Molly's mouth went into ventriloquist mode so no one would know she was talking about them. "That little girl with the blue jacket...she belongs to the first guy on line. The two boys at the end, they look like brothers, their dad's the big tall guy with the sunglasses. And the ten year old with the braces and the striped shirt, his father's the one holding the *Times*."

"How do you know that?" I said in amazement.

"Duh, it's not because they look alike, Sloane," Molly rolled her eyes. "Little Miss Blue Jacket and her dad are dressed up in freshly ironed clothes. They're either off to some party or there's some neat freak mom living under their roof. The two boys and Mr. Sunglasses are wearing flip-flops, they're probably going to the beach. And the boy with the braces, he and his dad live around the corner from me. That's why I'm so brilliant."

We both laughed.

"Was this idle conversation or were you asking for a reason?"

"I don't know," I sighed.

"Well, if you're asking if I would know whether you and your father looked like you came from the same family, the answer is definitely yes."

"Oh, really," I said dryly.

"You think I'm kidding?" Molly leaned back in her chair and folded her arms across her chest. "You two are actually very easy. First, you'd both put your sunglasses on the top of your head as soon as you walk in the store. Then you'd immediately split up. Your dad would head for the freezer for the milk and the juice while you'd stand on line, not wasting a second."

I smiled. She was right. Shopping with dad was like a military operation, organized, efficient and perfectly executed. I made fun of him but had to admit I also lost patience with customers who hadn't made a decision what kind of bagels they wanted by the time they got to the front of the line.

"You'd both order the same three sesame, three onion, whatever… no new flavors, God forbid, and then most of the time you'd come up with the exact change." She raised her eyebrows. "How am I doing?"

"You're terrific," I said with a grin.

"And lastly, neither of you would ever leave without smiling at the guy behind the counter and saying thank you. That definitely runs in families."

I took a sip of my hot chocolate.

"The truth is I think I'd have a tougher time being sure you and your mom were related than you and your dad."

We sat quietly for a while.

Finally Molly continued. "You say he's like a zombie now. Maybe shocking him a little is exactly what he needs to get him going. So what if he gets mad, it won't be the first time. Maybe he'll be relieved, did you ever think of that?" She looked directly in my eyes. "Please Sloane, talk to him."

CHAPTER SEVENTEEN

"Honey, do me a favor. Bring this tray out to your father."

It was Memorial Day and Mom insisted we celebrate with a barbecue. Emma was in the kitchen helping with the salad and Mom was searching through her cookbooks trying to find something new to accompany the traditional hot dogs, hamburgers and chicken.

"How does vegetable polenta sound?" she offered.

Emma and I looked at each other.

"We'd rather have corn on the cob, right Sloane?"

"You two duke it out," I said, picking up the tray and starting for the backyard. "As long as I have my burger, I'm happy."

"Stay out there with him for a while," Mom called out. "I'm sure he'd like the company."

I was sure he wouldn't. Last year he loved the whole manly routine of cooking outdoors, making a big show of flourishing the huge spatula and fork Mom bought him. He'd brag about the skill involved in making Emma's hamburger well done and mine medium rare and having them both ready at exactly the same time. I knew Mom hoped maybe he'd find some pleasure in barbecuing again today.

As I walked toward him, I could tell that was not happening. He stood stiffly, hands in his pockets, waiting for the coals to heat up.

"Here's the rest of the food, Dad," I said, putting the tray down on the bench next to the grill. "You're standing there like you're waiting for a train."

He turned and looked at me with no expression. "A train?" he said blankly, his pinched face looking even pinchier in the sunlight.

"A train," I repeated. "It's a joke, Dad. With your hands in your pockets you looked like…"

"Oh, I see," he said absent-mindedly. He stared at the tray.

"Need some help?" I asked, concerned if he spaced out any more, he'd forget to put the food on the grill.

"If you want," he said flatly, "you could take care of cooking this stuff."

I felt a twinge of something gearing me up. "Nah, I'll just stand by and watch the master," I replied.

The master, I thought grimly. He was the master all right, but only as long as he stayed inside the small world he ruled. When that world was upended, first with his illness and then with me finding out about mom's insemination, it completely unnerved him.

He took his hands out of his pockets and opened the cover of the grill. It would be a while before it was hot enough to put on the food. He exhaled loudly through his mouth, the delay exasperating him.

Suddenly, I couldn't take it any more. The silence. The defeat. Words rushed out of my mouth so fast it was as if we both heard them for the first time.

"Dad, don't get angry but you should be taking the antidepressants the doctor recommended. He's not convinced it's because of the leukemia that you have no energy." I gulped. "And it's not the leukemia's fault that nothing makes you happy any more." Then I took a deep breath and went for broke. "I don't understand how you could survive what you survived, all that suffering, and then give up."

Dad's face hardened and he looked away. His whole body deflated. Then he let out a breath and his shoulders slumped forward.

"Happy pills are not for me." His eyes were dark and unreadable and his voice was without emotion.

"Prove it. Take the medication for one month. If it doesn't help, stop. Just do something. You took chemo to fight the cancer. How's that different from taking other medication to fight your depression?" I paused. "You've been miserable for months already. What do you have to lose?"

He didn't answer.

"It doesn't make you less of a man if you take a pill to help you to feel better," I said quietly. "It makes you less of a man if you don't care enough about your family to even try."

He smiled feebly. "Since when are you so concerned?" He took the tray off the bench and sat down.

"Since when am I concerned?" I exploded. "I've been way beyond concerned every single day since you got sick." I sat down heavily beside him. "You're unbelievable, you know that?" I went on, unable to stop. "You're on my mind all the time. Half the time I'm worried sick that you're not getting well fast enough. The other half, I'm so angry at you for not trying harder. I have stuff I want to talk to you about…I have to talk to you about… but when I see how weak and down you are, I'm afraid to say anything that might upset you." I stopped to catch my breath.

"OK," Dad murmured, "Talk. I'm ready." He crossed his legs and rested his arm on the top of the bench.

I swallowed hard. "Right now?"

He nodded. "Let's get this over with," he said, his voice shaking a little. "It's time."

My mind was racing. How do I begin?

"You know what?" he said suddenly, "I'll start." He leaned forward and looked deep into my eyes. "Just promise to listen with an open mind."

I watched as he struggled to stand. He nervously started pacing back and forth in front of me.

"It's true what you said that night," he began. "I was devastated to find out I was the reason your mother was having such a hard time becoming pregnant. Starting a family was the most important thing to us. Your grandparents couldn't wait. I'd never even heard of anyone having a low sperm count, let alone that it could happen to me." He looked up at the sky. "We considered adoption but I couldn't bear that, because of my ego, your mother would never experience what it would be like to be pregnant and give birth."

I noticed his palms were sweating.

"I'm not going to lie to you. At first, I hated the whole idea of artificial insemination. You know me, giving up control of even the smallest part of my life is murder…but it would have been selfish and wrong not to at least try to deal with it."

He sat back down. "After you were conceived, the hardest part for me was over. I hardly thought about where the sperm came from. I convinced myself that as long as no one knew, as long as I never had to talk about it, I could handle the rest."

My heartbeat slowed.

"And then you were born." He smiled faintly.

"From the moment I saw you in the delivery room, I never felt like anything but your father. You were my daughter, you belonged to me. There was an immediate connection so strong, that I honestly believed there'd be no reason to tell you otherwise."

He closed his eyes and rubbed them. "Until Emma was born."

I wanted to touch him but I couldn't move.

"I panicked at first. Then I convinced myself that lots of siblings look different and plenty of biological kids don't resemble their dads at all." He sighed. "I was relieved when Emma came out looking less like me than you did." He shook his head. "But that was the end of my guilt-free days. You were four years old and as many times as I rehearsed in my head what I might've said, as gently and positively as humanly possible, I couldn't. How could I say I wasn't your real father, when I truly believed I was?" He laughed nervously. "I practiced the simplest of explanations…'Daddy couldn't make babies so we found a man who helped,' a dozen times… but couldn't get it out. So I said nothing."

I was breathing more evenly.

"How's the fire coming?" Mom yelled from the kitchen window.

"Fine," Dad and I yelled back in unison.

"I just…" I began.

"No, no, let me finish," Dad said firmly. He looked down in his lap and clasped his hands. "If I had acted responsibly, if I was as OK about this insemination thing as I should have been, you wouldn't have had to go through this all by yourself. I should have been there to help you. To find out you have a biological father somewhere out there, and on top of that, to have me acting like such a jerk…" He looked at me for the first time. "I am very sorry about that." Dad cleared his throat.

"Now that you know the truth, I'd expect you to do what you have to do."

The naked ache in his eyes cut me to the bone. Finally the words I waited so long to hear… and I didn't know what to say.

"I would expect you to try to get in touch with this…guy. If you're anything like me…and you are…," his voice grew thick, "you'll have to."

We sat there without speaking.

"Maybe they have some support groups to direct kids like you. You know, to guide you in the right direction."

"You just said it, Dad, I'm like you. The group thing's not for me."

He looked at me warily. "Don't be wise."

"I'm not," I said seriously. "If I can talk to you, I don't need a support group."

"And what about the sperm donor, you are going to try to find him, right?"

Before I could answer he went on.

"I don't mind telling you, I was a little intimidated by how smart this guy was…some kind of genius, I think your mother said. I would look at you sometimes when you did so well at school or you acted so maturely, and wonder…would you be so terrific a kid if you were made from my sperm?"

Incredible. My father, Coach Davis, so unsure of himself that he attributed the best parts of me to a stranger.

"Oh Daddy," I said, my eyes filling with tears.

He opened his arms and I rested my head on his shoulder as I had done hundreds of times through the years.

"Your sister's marrow made it possible for me to live," he whispered. "but if I thought I lost you, I don't know that I would want to."

"Prove it," I said sniffling, as I pulled away to look at his face.

"Prove what?"

"Prove that you want to live. Take the stupid anti-depressant. Start exercising again. Answer the telephone."

Dad shook his head. "It's not that easy."

"So what," I interrupted. "Since when in your life did you not try something because it wasn't easy? What did you tell me when I was afraid to ring doorbells and sell Girl Scout cookies? You said that a salesman's job began when the customer said no. I learned that lesson. I'm warning you, I've only just begun...."

He cracked a small smile.

I knew I had him.

"You're the first one to talk about the power of desire," I pleaded. "All I'm asking is that you desire to feel better."

"All right. All right. I can't argue against my own spiel. I'll try your wonder drugs. I owe you at least that."

"And exercising?"

"And the phone," he promised. He cupped his hand under my chin and lifted my face. "Damn," he said softly as he kissed the top of my head. "If you're not my daughter, I'll eat this chicken raw."

A few weeks later, Mom, Emma and I were sitting on the living room floor trying to put a bow on the treadmill we bought Dad for Father's Day.

"He better use it," Mom warned as I finished attaching our cards to the box. "This will be an expensive coat rack if he doesn't."

"He will," I said confidently. "Since he saw everybody from work at his high school's end of the year party, I think he's ready to start getting back into shape."

"Sloane's right, he is getting better," Emma chimed in. "He kisses me good night now, just like he used to."

"And all of a sudden he won't let go of the television remote. It's like he's waking up from a long winter's nap," I said, only half kidding. "For a few months there I got to watch whatever I wanted." I shook my head. "It's great to have him back, though, even if his watching three baseball games at the same time can drive a person crazy."

"Yes, it is good," Mom said simply. She looked at me. "You had a lot to do with his change of heart, you know that, don't you?"

I smiled. "We all did."

"He still has a long way to go," she reminded me. "The crystal ball is still cloudy. Dad's going to need our prayers and a huge helping of luck for the rest of his life."

We all busied ourselves, chasing away thoughts of a recurrence of leukemia. I wasn't taking his return to good health for granted, but what sense would it make that in one year I could lose him, find him, only to lose him again?

This year I was angry and less than honest with everyone I loved. I kept secrets because I feared I'd have to fight...and I hate to fight... if I told the truth. But swallowing the facts numbs you out. The truth becomes a silent stowaway, taking up space where self confidence belongs. Now I feel so grateful, realizing everything good that happened to me happened only after I expressed how I felt.

This Father's Day was definitely one to give thanks. And as my mind flashed on the blond chemistry major who attended the University of Pennsylvania, I thanked him too. For the gift of life, probably for my love of the ocean, and definitely for the color of my eyes. The knowledge he exists is a part of me, like the scar on my leg where I fell off my bike...always there but fading and unremarkable. One day, maybe I'll check out an old photograph. Maybe we'll meet, who knows? Until then, I wished him a Happy Father's Day, one I just had a feeling he deserved.

Purchase other Black Rose Writing titles at www.blackrosewriting.com/books and use promo code PRINT to receive a 20% discount.

BLACK ROSE
writing™

CPSIA information can be obtained at www.ICGtesting.com
Printed in the USA
BVOW01s0939090115

382585BV00011B/126/P

9 781612 964638